Also by Andrew Porter

The Disappeared

Alfred A. Knopf
New York
2023

The
Disappeared

STORIES

ANDREW PORTER

THIS IS A BORZOI BOOK PUBLISHED BY ALFRED A. KNOPF

www.aaknopf.com

Knopf, Borzoi Books, and the colophon are registered trademarks
of Penguin Random House LLC.

Several of these stories first appeared, in slightly different form, in the following
publications: "Austin" in *Ploughshares*; "Vines" in *Southern Review*; "Cello"
and "Jimena" in *Narrative*; "Rhinebeck" and "Breathe" in *Epoch*; "Chili" and
"Pozole" in *Chicago Quarterly Review*; "Bees" in *Colorado Review*; "Silhouettes"
in *Boulevard*; "Cigarettes" in *Sonora Review*; "The Empty Unit" in *New Letters*.

Library of Congress Cataloging-in-Publication Data
Names: Porter, Andrew, 1972– author.
Title: The disappeared / Andrew Porter.
Description: First Edition. | New York : Alfred A. Knopf, 2023.
Identifiers: LCCN 2022037102 (print) | LCCN 2022037103 (ebook) |
ISBN 9780593534304 (hardcover) | ISBN 9780593534311 (ebook)
Subjects: LCGFT: Novels.
Classification: LCC PS3616.O75 D57 2023 (print) | LCC PS3616.O75 (ebook) |
DDC 813/.6—dc23/eng/20220812
LC record available at https://lccn.loc.gov/2022037102
LC ebook record available at https://lccn.loc.gov/2022037103

Jacket photograph by Vanzyst / Shutterstock
Jacket design by John Gall

Manufactured in the United States of America

First Edition

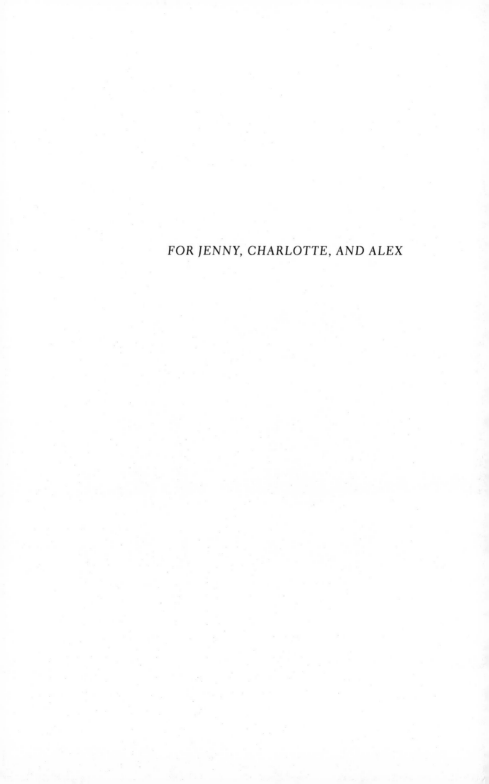

FOR JENNY, CHARLOTTE, AND ALEX

CONTENTS

The Disappeared

Austin

The other night at a party in Westlake Hills, just outside of Austin, I stepped outside to get some air and found a group of my old friends sitting around a fire pit in the backyard, smoking cigarettes. It was a strange sight, not only because I hadn't seen most of these people in several years, but also because they were all still smoking, almost as if they had been frozen there in time, while I had been off somewhere else, getting married and having children and getting older. It was close to one o'clock in the morning by then, and my wife, Laura, had long since left the party. The air that night was brisk, and everyone was huddled around the fire, hugging their knees, holding their windbreakers close to their chests.

I sat down in one of the free chairs and raised my beer to the group, and everyone smiled and then someone, I think it was Mitch Allen, said that they should really ask me the question—that, as a father, I might have a different perspective on things. Aside from Mitch, there was Mitch's wife, Julie, Evan Benoit, and Greg and Debra Hull, who were married but still childless. Everyone there was at least forty-five years old, I realized, and yet I was the only one with kids.

"What we were talking about was something that happened last year to one of Evan's friends," Mitch said. "This guy Callen."

Evan pulled out a cigarette from his pack and shook his head. "If you're going to tell it again, I'm going to need another beer."

"I'm not going to tell it again," Mitch said. "I'm just going to give him the short version."

Mitch handed his pack of cigarettes to me, but I waved him away. "Eight years nicotine-free," I said, maybe a little too proudly. Everyone looked at me.

"Bullshit," Julie said. "I saw you smoking last summer at—where was it?"

"Julie," I said. "I don't think I've seen you in close to seven years."

Julie squinted her eyes, as if unsure of where she was at the moment. Everyone there was drunk, but Julie was perhaps a little further gone than the rest of us.

"Okay," Mitch said, lighting a cigarette himself. "Back to the story, okay? Check this out."

But the story Mitch told made little sense. He kept stopping and starting, revising what he'd just said, filling in background information that he should have mentioned before he began, checking with Evan to make sure that what he was saying was accurate, all the while taking long sips from his 40-oz can of beer. The whole scene reminded me of college, which was where I'd met most of the people there—everyone but Evan Benoit, who had fallen into our circle later. Anyway, the gist of the story was this. Evan's friend Callen had come home one night to find an intruder in his house. The intruder was a teenager, a little taller than Callen himself, but scrawny. It had been dark, though, and Callen hadn't been able to see anything but the vague shape of this kid in his hallway. His first thought had been to run, but then he'd remembered his girlfriend asleep in the bedroom, so he'd gone at the kid, run at him, not realizing he was a kid, and all pumped up on adrenaline, he'd somehow managed to kill him by ramming his head into the doorway of the bathroom.

The details of the story were pretty hazy, Mitch explained, because the guy that Evan knew had left Austin shortly after, had quit his job at UT, where he'd been teaching in the Department of Economics as an adjunct instructor, and was now pretty much incommunicado. As for the girlfriend, she'd tried to go with him wherever he went—Albuquerque, Evan thought—but he'd refused to let her. And of course there hadn't been any charges because it was perfectly legal to kill an intruder who had trespassed on your property, regardless of whether that person was armed or not—at least in the state of Texas.

"But look, that's not even the point," Mitch said. "The point is that this guy—Callen, right?—he's practically suicidal over this. He's pretty much checked out of life completely."

"Well, he did murder someone," Debra said. "Technically, I mean."

"In some people's eyes, yes," Mitch said. "In other people's eyes it was self-defense." Mitch looked at me then. "So that's the question, okay, and maybe as a father you can shed a little light on this, okay, maybe looking at it from the perspective of the kid's parents. I mean this kid was like, what—fifteen, maybe sixteen?"

"Fifteen." Evan nodded.

I shook my head. I'd left my coat inside and now had a sudden desire to retrieve it. Everyone else around the fire was just smoking quietly. They looked somber, like they'd all heard this story maybe one too many times. Evan smiled at me plaintively.

"Maybe we should talk about something else," he said.

We'd all convened here to celebrate the birthday of another friend, Daniel Herron, who had moved back to the area after a five- or six-year respite out in California. After Daniel had left, Laura and I had started hanging out a little more with some of Laura's other friends—her crowd from work and some of the women in her continuing-education class—and then we'd had the kids, Toby and June, one right after the other, and suddenly we felt kind of exiled from the old crowd, not because we didn't miss them, or didn't want to see them, but because we couldn't afford babysitters and didn't have family in the area to help us watch the kids. We'd still go out with them—maybe once or twice a month—but pretty soon it became easier for us to hang out at the houses of other couples like us, couples with kids, and I pretty much fell out of touch with Evan and Mitch and the rest of them.

It often made me feel sad to think of this, and I often felt guilty, but when I'd see their updates on Facebook—the concerts they were still going to, the late-night selfies taken in various nightclubs around the city—I felt as far away from them as if I'd moved to another country. They had managed to preserve their youth, while I had given in to the widening waistline, the boat shoes, the gray hair in my beard.

And yet, here was a familiar scene playing out before me—a late-night ethical dilemma, something straight out of Dostoevsky, and better still, it had happened to someone one of us knew—and yet I couldn't bring myself to play along with them. What I wanted to say was that I'd somehow lost sight of how to discern things like right and wrong and that when it came to matters like murder and death, it was all just sad to me. It wasn't about being justified or not. It was about something very sad that had happened to two human beings and their families. Beyond that, there was not much to say.

I didn't say any of this though. Instead, I just excused myself to the bathroom, promising Mitch I'd give him an answer upon my return—a father's take on what he'd just described—but somehow when I got out to the kitchen, I realized I wouldn't be going back. Something about the conversation had rattled me, depressed me. I looked out through the sliding glass doors at my friends, sitting around the fire pit with their cigarettes. I'd known most of these people close to twenty years, and yet at that moment I barely recognized them. I fixed myself a drink, and then, without saying goodbye to anyone—there were only a few people still sitting around the family room and kitchen—I walked down the hallway and out the front door.

At home, I found my wife, Laura, asleep on the couch. She'd come home before me—to pay the sitter and tuck in the kids—and now she was lying there, fully clothed, on the living room couch, her body wrapped in a blanket. I walked over to her and sat down beside her in the dim light and then put my hand on her leg. In the other room, I could hear the faint sound of music playing, something light and acoustic. After a moment, Laura stirred and looked up, blinking at me, squinting, as if she didn't recognize who I was.

"What are you doing out here?" I asked.

"Huh?"

"Why are you sleeping on the couch?"

She rubbed her eyes and sat up. "June had a nightmare," she said and pushed the blanket off her legs. "Something horrific again. I read her a book, and then we watched some TV, and then—I don't know."

"You put her to bed?"

"I must have," she said and looked around the room. "I think I had too much wine at the party. I shouldn't have driven home."

"Do you want me to check on her?"

"Yes." She nodded.

Our house is small, small enough that it's not hard to wake someone up at night simply by walking around the hardwood floors, and so I slipped off my shoes and walked quietly in my socks toward my daughter's room.

Inside, I found her fast asleep, her arms wrapped around her pillow, her body curved into the fetal position. She had just turned four years old—she was a year younger than our son, Toby—and there was very little about the world that upset her, very little that frightened her; and yet, she'd been having these dreams lately, these horrific dreams that troubled us. She'd describe them to us in exhaustive detail, almost as if she was describing a movie she'd seen or a book that she'd read. They were invariably dark, disturbing, filled with violent imagery and premonitory warnings, filled with what she liked to call signs. I had no idea what to make of them or where they'd come from. She was an otherwise happy child, described by her teachers as well adjusted, sweet. She had a generous spirit, a kind heart. How these other thoughts had entered her mind was a mystery to me.

I sat down beside her on the bed and turned on her table lamp, and then I leaned down and kissed her gently on the forehead. The room was quiet, silent except for the distant whir of the white-noise machine that Laura had bought for her last year, a muffled, staticky sound, and I sat there for a while, listening to it, mesmerized by the hum of this machine, staring at my daughter's face, wondering what type of dark thoughts were passing behind her eyes.

. . .

Back in the living room, I found Laura still sitting on the couch, this time holding a glass of wine. She'd been having her own sleep troubles lately—terrible bouts of insomnia followed by short periods of intense dreaming—and the only thing that seemed to remedy this was wine, several glasses of it each night before bed.

For almost a year after June was born, she'd barely been able to sleep, rarely more than two or three hours a night. She was exhausted all the time, and her exhaustion fueled her worries, which were numerous and vague, mostly worries related to the children and their health, their well-being, their safety. She'd read on the internet about some strange disease or some child development issue, and then she'd see evidence of this disease or this issue in our children. It got to the point where our pediatrician had to say something to her explicitly, where he had to get me involved.

Now she did her worrying privately, spent her evenings watching TV, drinking wine, sometimes doing the crossword puzzle. I tried to give her as much space as possible.

"Everything okay?" I said now, as I sat down beside her on the couch.

She nodded. "June's sleeping?"

"She is."

"Good." She picked up her wineglass and took a sip. "I don't really know what's going on with me tonight actually. Something in the air, I guess."

"Did you have fun at the party?"

"No. Did you?"

"I don't know," I said. "It was kind of weird, you know, seeing all those people."

She nodded.

I thought then of telling her the story about the intruder, the story that Mitch Allen had told me, though I don't know why this thought occurred to me. This was exactly the type of story that would set her off, that would send her into a panic. So instead, I mentioned a couple of our other old friends, Monica and Stacey, whom I'd spoken to earlier that night. They had a son who was around Toby's age.

"Did they tell you what happened to Noah?" Laura said.

"No," I said.

"Really?" she said. "I would have thought they'd mention it. It's so sad."

I could tell from her expression that she wanted to talk about this—that she wanted to talk about whatever had happened to their son, Noah—but at that moment I didn't want to know.

"I think I'm going to make myself something to drink," I said. "Do you want anything?"

She shook her head. "I just want to sleep."

In the kitchen, I fixed myself a gin and tonic in the dark, using the light from the open refrigerator door to guide me, and then I brought my glass back into the living room and sat down with Laura for a while, sat there and watched her sleep. Her eyes were closed now, and I could see her chest moving up and down slowly.

In the other room, I could hear the sound of classical music coming from the stereo, a polonaise by Chopin that I recognized from my youth, and after a while, I decided to pick up my drink and walk in there. This was the family room, I guess, the room with the TV and the stereo and all of our books lined up against the walls. Like every other room in the house, Laura kept it dimly lit at night—she has a sensitivity to light—and I'd always enjoyed sitting in it with a book and a glass of wine, sometimes a mixed drink. These were the simple pleasures of my life these days—the way I spent those two or three hours in the evenings after work, just after the kids had fallen asleep. Did I want more? I sometimes believed I did, but at that moment, I was content to simply sit there and listen to this music, to the strange poetry of it, to hold a drink in my hand, and to know that I was in my own house and that I was safe here, that down the hallway my children were asleep in their beds.

Outside I could hear the occasional sound of a car passing, young people shouting things into the air. When did I become the person who listened to such sounds and not the person who made them? These were the types of questions I often asked myself late at night, as I sat here in this chair, sipping on my drink, feeling at peace, but also somehow adrift, somehow disconnected from things, as if I'd been untethered from some larger purpose. There was always the sense of a shadow looming just beyond the wall, the hum of a greater absence. There was always that sense that something I'd once owned had been lost, or left behind, abandoned. How could I explain such feelings to my wife? I closed my eyes and returned to the Chopin. It was a different melody now. A nocturne. Delicate, lyrical, soft.

I don't know what happened after that. I must have drifted off because the next thing I remember was Laura shaking me awake, saying that she had heard something out in our backyard. We have a laundry that attaches to our garage—a kind of inconvenient eccentricity of our house—and often, at night, Laura will claim that she hears things out there. It's true that once or twice I've gone outside and found the door ajar, but I've never actually seen anyone in there. Our backyard is surrounded on all sides by a fence—a fairly tall fence—and so one would have to be pretty brazen to climb over the fence and then try to access our garage or laundry room, even under the cover of darkness, but even so, I could see that Laura was serious. She was holding a flashlight in her hand and staring at me intently.

"And another thing," she said. "The light's on in the laundry room. Did I mention that?"

"That's happened before," I said. "It was probably me."

"It wasn't on earlier," she said, "when I got home. I would have noticed."

"Are you sure?"

"Yes." She nodded.

I took the flashlight from her hand and stood up.

Out in the living room, I could see that she'd woken up the children and had them sit on the couch. They were bleary-eyed and barely conscious, our younger one, June, wrapped in a blanket, our older, Toby, dressed in his Cowboys pajamas. It was almost three o'clock in the morning.

I smiled at the kids and then put on my shoes again, and Laura shepherded me toward the kitchen and then out to the little hallway that led to the back deck. Of course, I was thinking about the story that Mitch had told earlier. I wondered what the chances were— hearing a story like that, and then living it out, being faced with a similar dilemma myself. I imagined them telling *that* story.

It was probably the unlikelihood of this scenario playing itself out that made me so certain I wouldn't find anyone out there in the garage or the laundry room, even with the light turned on, and in fact I didn't. Everything was just as it should have been. I turned off the light above the laundry room sink, and then stood there for a moment in the darkness, staring out through the little round window above the dryer. I could see the house about twenty yards away and the faces of my children and Laura framed in the kitchen window. I don't know why this suddenly frightened me, but it did. I realized that they were staring out at me but couldn't see me. They had no idea where I was.

I stood there for a moment longer, though, just staring at them, and that's when I felt what seemed at first to be a throbbing in my leg, but which turned out to be my cell phone buzzing, pulsing in my pocket, alerting me of an incoming text—or, in this case, a text that had been sent earlier that night from Mitch, my old friend, probably wondering why I hadn't returned from the bathroom, why I'd never come back to answer his question. I flipped open the phone but didn't look at the message. Instead I was focused on the house again, on the window, where my family had just now been standing. The window was empty now, their faces gone, and I wondered for a moment if I had imagined it, dreamed it. This had become such a ritual lately, this waking up at night to check on the backyard, the laundry, the garage, this inspecting of strange noises, this securing of windows, this strengthening of locks. This was all part of this new world we had entered, this new dream we had begun to dream. And yet, at times, there were still cracks in the dream, voices from the past that startled you, little winks from that other life, like that text message from Mitch that still glowed faintly on my phone. *What happened to you, buddy?* it read, in soft blue text. *Where did you go?*

Cigarettes

In the other life, the life before we had kids, I used to sometimes imagine us in some foreign city—Barcelona, Rome—sitting in a courtyard drinking espresso, smoking cigarettes, which we'd always smoked since we'd known each other and which I had imagined at that time we would always smoke for the rest of our lives. Our afternoons and mornings back then were quiet affairs, reading books, preparing for our classes, sometimes catching up on the news; our evenings, though, were what I looked forward to; the movement from coffee to wine, from dinner to after-dinner drinks and cigarettes out on the back deck, listening to music from our childhood, our teenage years, often having friends over for more drinks, more cigarettes, but always ending the evening together, in bed, or pressed together on the couch, our bodies entwined.

How were we to know back then that all of that would change—

that *that* would not be us forever, that after the first child the cigarettes would be gone forever, and after the second, the wine and late
nights? There would be the richness of our lives together now, the
love and goodness multiplied by two, more bodies in the house, more
laughter, more fun, but also, at the end of the day, less of us.

The other night when you were lying supine on the couch, the
kids in bed early for once, I snuck into the dining room in search
of the one pack of cigarettes I'd saved and hidden—the "emergency
pack" I had called it all those months when I was quitting—and was
surprised to find it still there, perfectly intact, sealed in a plastic bag-
gie, maybe a little old, but not totally stale yet, certainly smokeable.

I pulled out the shot glasses, put on some Nina Simone. I went
in search of the *orujo* my sister-in-law had brought us last year from
Spain. It was only eight o'clock and neither of us had classes the
next day. I was thinking that maybe we could take the *orujo* and the
cigarettes and the music out onto the back deck and maybe, I don't
know—I'm not really sure what I was thinking, but it didn't end up
mattering anyway because by the time I'd found the *orujo* and set up
the glasses on a tray and found a pack of matches for the cigarettes,
you were already fast asleep on the couch, your mouth wide open
as if you'd been in the middle of a sentence and forgotten what you
wanted to say.

You looked beautiful, though, even with your mouth open, and I
stood there for a moment, in the dim light of our family room, watching you, wondering whether or not to wake you.

In the end, I decided to just let you sleep and took the cigarettes
and the *orujo* out onto the back deck by myself. It was a cold night,
unseasonably cold for San Antonio, and I was shivering by the time
I'd poured myself a half-shot of the *orujo* and pulled out the cigarettes and the matches.

There's always that fear of starting up again, of falling back into the hole of nicotine addiction, but that's not what I was thinking about then, and that's not why I started crying. I'm not really sure why I started crying, actually, because I *don't* cry, as you know, and had not cried in probably five or six years, maybe longer, and so I'm not really sure what it was that brought it on, maybe just the overwhelming fatigue of our lives lately, all the long days finally catching up with me, or maybe it was the strength of the alcohol in the *orujo*, or maybe just the cold and the sight of you through the sliding glass doors, fast asleep, that sense of something being lost, or maybe it was simply the fact that when I lit up that cigarette after all those years—it had been four, I realized only then—I knew before I even inhaled, before I even pulled the smoke into my lungs, that it had been a mistake, that I had been wrong to do this, and that of course the cigarette—stale and dried out and shriveled from all that time alone—would taste nothing at all like I remembered.

Vines

Just last year I discovered that I had an entire closet filled with things that I had no practical use for, things that I had accumulated over the years but wasn't ready to part with yet. One of the things in this closet was a small painting by an ex-girlfriend of mine who had since died of cancer. The ex-girlfriend's name was Maya, and she had died two years earlier at the age of forty-three. The painting was one of the last paintings she made before she stopped making paintings altogether.

At the time that Maya gave me this painting we were living together in a small garage apartment on the south side of San Antonio, just a few blocks up from the old Pioneer Flour Mills, an area of the city called King William that was famous for its historic homes. The home that our apartment was attached to, though, wasn't historic. It was just a modest one-story house owned by a man named Lionel Merritt, who had purchased it in the late eighties when he'd taught printmaking out at the University of Texas at San Antonio. Lionel had kept the house even after his daughter had left and his wife had died and he had retired from teaching. He had three bedrooms in the main house and a large studio out at the far end of the backyard that he let Maya use in the evenings.

Lionel did his own work in the early mornings, sometimes waking as early 4:00 a.m. to get started. He liked to work when it was still dark out, he said, when he was still only half-awake, when he still had one foot in his own dreams. As the sun gradually rose in the large oval-shaped window at the far end of the studio, he'd feel himself waking up, returning to the world of the living, as he put it, and by the time the sun had fully risen he'd be winding down and getting ready to stop.

When I'd come down from our garage apartment in the morning, I'd often find him sitting out there on one of the small metal chairs outside the studio, smoking a cigarette and drinking a cup of coffee, his work for the day already done.

Back in his youth, Lionel had made a bit of a name for himself as a printmaker, but now he was doing mostly watercolors, figurative paintings, many of them sexual in nature and often strange. He kept these pieces locked away in a large locker at the back of the studio, but occasionally he'd leave a few out to dry and Maya and I would come across them when she went in there in the evenings to work. I remember the first time we came across one of his nudes sitting out on a large, white worktable. The figure in the painting was turned away from the viewer, but I could tell right away who it was. It was a girl we'd seen going into his studio in the early mornings, two or three times a week over the past month—a blond girl, probably no older than twenty-five, with long limbs and a striking face. A sort of sun-drenched beauty. Lionel had never introduced us to this girl, and so we'd spent a lot of time in the late evenings drinking beer and speculating about who she was: A wayward daughter? A niece? A former student? A lover? It was like a game we played, and Maya would often get carried away with her theories, piecing together evidence from all of the things she'd observed. *Sometimes she smokes with him,* she'd say, picking up her beer. *She probably wouldn't smoke with him if she was his daughter, right? He wouldn't let her.*

But now, with the nude sitting right there before us, all of these theories seemed to go out the window.

"Probably just a model," I said. "Someone he's paying, right? Don't artists do that?"

"I don't think she's just a model," Maya said, picking up the sheet and staring closely at it. "I can tell. He's definitely sleeping with her."

"How do you know?"

She shrugged. "I can just tell."

"He's, like, sixty years old," I said.

"I know," she said, "but he's a youthful sixty."

"You think he's youthful?"

"I'm just saying he's a handsome man, you know, and famous— locally, at least."

I stared at her. "You're starting to worry me."

"Please," she said. "I'm just saying I remember what it was like to be twenty-three or twenty-four years old and the power of an older man like that—especially when you're starting out as an artist and seeking all that validation."

"You think she's an artist?"

"I don't know," she said. "Probably. Don't you get that vibe?"

At the time, Maya had recently turned thirty-one, and though she could have easily passed for twenty-three or twenty-four herself, I knew she didn't feel that way. She had recently started complaining about all of the tiny lines at the corners of her eyes, the soreness in her joints, the sunspots on her arms. *I'm turning into an old lady right before your eyes,* she'd say and then she'd drop her head dramatically into my chest and ask me to hold her. We had been together for almost two years at that point, the longest I had ever been with one woman and the longest she had ever been with one man. We weren't talking about marriage or anything, but we weren't avoiding the subject either. When people would ask us about it, we'd look at each other knowingly and then one of us would smile and say, *Who knows? Stranger things have happened, right?*

That evening, though, I could tell that something was bothering Maya. She seemed lost in thought. There was something about the girl in the watercolor that had unnerved her.

Later that night, as we lay in bed, passing a cigarette back and forth, she said, "It's disgusting. Don't you think?"

"What?"

"Next door," she said. "What's going on with Lionel and that girl."

I picked up the beer I'd brought in from the kitchen and took a sip. It was close to a hundred degrees that evening—mid-July in San Antonio, the heat refusing to burn off. Above us, the ceiling fan was running at full speed.

"It's disgusting," I said. "Yes."

Maya slid up next to me in the bed and took the beer from my hand, pressing the sweating bottle against her cheek.

"I want to know who she is," she said.

"Why?"

"I don't know," she said, and then she looked out the window in the direction of the studio, though it was too dark to see anything. "I just do."

. . .

At the beginning of the summer Maya and I had driven all the way out to California to see my parents, and on the drive back, somewhere between Las Cruces and El Paso, she told me that she'd been thinking a lot about an article she'd read about an artist named Sara Genn. Genn had talked about the importance of an artist having a studio close by—a few paces from the house or in the loft next door. It was very important, this artist felt, for one's art to always be available.

Maya had always worked out of a studio on the south side of San Antonio, a communal space that she had access to twenty-four hours a day but which also required her to drive at least twenty minutes each way every time she wanted to work. More and more often she'd found herself opting not to work simply because of the drive.

The other week, though, an old professor of hers from graduate school had brought up the local printmaker Lionel Merritt and mentioned that Lionel often rented out the small apartment above his garage as well as a portion of his studio space to local artists. He'd given her Lionel's number, and when she called him he told her that the apartment had just become available.

We were driving through the flat, barren deserts of West Texas at this point, and I could tell that Maya was building up to something. She said that right before we'd left for our trip she'd stopped by to see the apartment and it was perfect. The only problem was the rent. If she was going to live there, she'd need to get a roommate.

At that point we'd talked casually about living together, but never seriously. We both lived in small apartments less than a mile apart. We could walk to each other anytime we wanted. It was a nice arrangement.

"I would never pressure you," she said.

"I know."

"You can take some time to think about it."

"I don't need to," I said, and then I reached over and took her hand, the sun setting in the distance. "I think this'll be a good thing."

And so far, it had been. In the mornings Maya would leave for her job at the San Antonio Museum of Art, where she worked part-time in the protective services department, and I would leave for mine at the local coffee- and teahouse in our neighborhood, where I worked as a barista. In the evenings, we'd find each other in the small courtyard behind Lionel's house, where we'd share a couple of beers and sometimes a light salad before Maya would head into the studio to work.

Since we'd been here, Maya's work had been going well. She worked five to six hours each night, sometimes finishing up after I was already asleep in bed, and the work she was doing was good. Mostly abstract paintings inspired by her numerous trips to Mexico in the past few years. I could tell she was aware that she was doing good work and that this was a particularly fruitful time for her, maybe even a breakthrough period, so we didn't talk about the work she was doing and I didn't look at it unless she asked me to. There was something almost superstitious about it, like a baseball player on a hitting streak. We didn't want to jinx it.

Meanwhile, I spent most of my evenings sitting out in the courtyard reading books, catching up on all of those classics I'd always meant to get to but never had had time to read: *The Brothers Karamazov, Madame Bovary, Effi Briest.* The courtyard was surrounded on all sides by various desert plants—salvias and yuccas and cacti—and at the far end of the yard there was a tall metal fence covered with bougainvillea and other flowering vines that spilled over into the back alley.

Sometimes, in the evenings, Lionel would come out to join me for a cigarette and a glass of wine. He never drank beer, only wine, and he always brought his own bottle and glasses for us to use.

Maya had been right about Lionel's looks—they were youthful and refined, almost feminine, his eyes very pale, his skin smooth and tan, his thick hair only slightly graying but otherwise blond. He liked to wear light, flowing shirts and linen pants, dark sandals, or sometimes no shoes at all.

When he'd sit down, he'd always smile at me knowingly, as if we were in cahoots about something, and then he'd uncork the bottle and pour us both a glass.

I knew that the wines he was sharing with me were very good, though I knew little about wine, and occasionally he'd talk about them and where they'd come from and who the vintner was. Mostly, though, he liked to talk about himself and the work he was doing and where he was planning to travel next and who he had just met recently who had impressed him. It didn't take long to get the sense that Lionel held himself in very high regard. No shortage of ego there. Still, there were moments when he also seemed suddenly vulnerable and lost, lonely—especially when he talked about his second wife, who had died three years earlier, or about his daughter, who was currently living in Brooklyn and not talking to him.

Maya always encouraged me to ask him about the girl who stopped by in the mornings, just to see what he would say, just to see what I could find out, but I could never bring myself to do it. I knew that if he'd wanted me to know about her, he would have told me by now. So instead I'd ask him about himself or about his early life as an artist in San Antonio, and occasionally I'd even talk about myself or about Maya and our relationship.

Early on, Lionel had assumed that I was an artist of some sort, and when I'd told him later that I wasn't, really—that I was just a barista—he remained skeptical.

"But what do you *love* to do," he'd said to me one evening, as he poured us both another glass.

"I don't know," I said. "I guess I'm still figuring that out."

"How old are you?" he said.

"Thirty-one."

He nodded and sipped his wine. I could tell that he wanted to say something then, but he didn't. Instead, he put out his cigarette. After a moment, he said, "What did you major in in college?"

"Film," I said. "But I didn't finish."

"Why not?"

"I don't know," I said. "I never really figured that out. I think I just lost interest."

He nodded again. "But you did want to make films at one point?"

"No," I said. "I was more into the theory side of things. At least for a while."

He put down his glass. "Well," he said. "There's a life to be had there, too, right?"

"There is," I said. "Just not my life."

He laughed lightly, and then motioned for me to hand him one of the cigarettes from my pack, which I did. After he'd lit the cigarette, he looked at me for a long time and smiled.

Then he reached over casually, almost like he was reaching for my glass, and took my hand. It was a strange moment. He held it for a short time and then he looked at me very seriously and said, "You know, if you ever need anything, I'm right next door, okay?"

"Okay," I said.

"I'm serious," he said. "Anything at all."

"Okay," I said. "Thanks."

Then he stood up and turned around and headed back inside.

.   .   .

That night, when Maya got home from working, I decided not to mention anything about Lionel and our strange little moment in the courtyard. I could tell that she'd had a bad night, that she'd lost a little bit of that inner force that had driven her in recent weeks. She complained about feeling boxed in, uninspired, frustrated. She said that ever since she'd seen that painting of the girl she'd lost her focus.

She said Lionel had somehow sexualized the space and it had thrown her off.

"Plus, his paintings are so good."

"So are yours."

"Not like that, though."

"I like yours better, personally."

"Of course you do," she said. "You're a loyal man."

"Even if I didn't know you," I said. "I'm serious." And I was. I loved the work that Maya had been doing since we arrived there, loved all of her work, in fact, but especially these latest paintings, which seemed inspired by something very primitive and instinctual, something very human inside of her.

I told her all of this that night, but she remained discouraged. She was wearing the baggy overalls she always painted in and a tight tank top, and after she'd finished her beer, she took them both off right there in the middle of the kitchen and walked into the bathroom to shower. I went into the bedroom and turned on the jazz station she liked.

When she got out of the shower a few minutes later, she came over to the bed, her body wrapped in a towel, and lay down.

"I thought of at least three things I want to say to Lionel the next time I see him," she said.

"Okay."

"Only I'll never say them, so what's the point?"

"That he's a pig," I said.

"Well, yes, that. I was actually going to use the word predator."

"That he's overrated."

"Yes. Only he's not. He's actually doing some of his best work right now."

"What else?"

"I don't know," she said. "It's stupid. Why do I hate him so much? I should be grateful to him for giving us this space, right? We have a nice life here."

She rolled over onto her side and looked at me. Then she pulled off her towel slowly, so that I could see her body.

"Do you think I'm as beautiful as that girl?"

"What are you doing?"

"Just answer me."

"Of course," I said and kept my eyes on hers. "What's going on with you?"

"I don't know." She sighed. "I think that turning thirty last year really fucked me up."

"Yeah," I said. "I think so."

"Be nice."

I eased up close to her. "You're the most beautiful woman I've ever known personally," I said and took her hand. "And definitely the most beautiful woman I've ever dated."

She looked at me then, briefly, before turning away and staring up at the ceiling. "I appreciate that," she said and closed her eyes. "You can't understand why, but I do."

At the end of the summer Maya would give me a series of three paintings that she'd painted in quick succession. A triptych. She knew that I was a big fan of the fourteenth-century Italian painter Giotto and specifically the frescoes he'd done in the Arena Chapel in Padua, and so she'd modeled these paintings after those of Giotto, perfectly catching the deep blues of Giotto's skies, the complex yet simply rendered religious themes.

Months later, after we'd broken up, she'd ask for this triptych back. She'd want to use it in her very first gallery show in San Francisco, and it would sell on the very first day to a doctor, who would then take it away to his private residence and hang it on a wall, never to be seen by either one of us again. But that July, as the heat was topping off in the triple digits every night, I remember her working on those paintings in the dim evening light of Lionel's studio. Even Lionel said something to me about the triptych one night while we were sitting out in the courtyard, having a glass of wine.

"She's in that rare space," he said. "I can tell."

I nodded.

"It's nice when that happens."

I looked back at the studio where I could see a light on in the window and knew Maya was working. After a week of feeling thwarted and discouraged, she'd hit her stride again.

"One's twenties are for figuring out what you want to do, I think. But one's thirties are when you do your best work."

"Is that when you did your best work?"

He nodded. "Without a doubt."

This seemed like a good opportunity to ask him about the girl who'd been stopping by in the mornings, the girl he'd been painting. He'd referred to her a few times in the past week as Caroline and implied that she was a protégé of sorts. I asked him if she was in the figuring-out stage still, and he just smiled.

"Oh no," he said. "Caroline came into the world fully formed as an artist. She's one of those rare breeds. She'll have a show in Houston by the end of the year, I'm sure."

"Really?"

"Oh yes. Definitely."

I looked at him. "You two seem close."

He smiled. "If you want to know if I'm sleeping with her, just ask me."

"Okay," I said. "Are you?"

"No." He laughed. "Of course not. She's probably half my age, Simon." He picked up his wineglass and took a long sip. "Plus," he said, "as maudlin as it may sound, I think I'm still in love with my wife." He looked down at his feet and rubbed them. Then he smiled at me, but there was something distant about the smile, forced, as there always seemed to be when he spoke about his wife.

After a moment, he put out his cigarette.

"Another?" he said, nodding at the bottle.

"No," I said. "That's okay." And then I stood up. "I think I'm probably done for the night."

Later that night, when Maya got home, I was lying in bed, listening to the radio—we didn't have a TV at the time—trying my best to fall asleep. The program I was listening to was called *Los Olvidados*, and it was about lost children in Guatemala. It had depressed me. When Maya came in, she went straight into the bathroom and turned on the shower. A few minutes later, she came out in just her towel and sat on the bed.

"It's late," I said.

"I was talking to Lionel."

"Yeah? What about?"

"Nothing, really," she said. And then she stood up and went over to the closet to get dressed.

As she put on her clothes, I told her a little about my conversation with Lionel earlier that night and how we were probably misreading what was going on with that girl, how he claimed to still be in love with his wife. I could hear Maya pull down a few of the boxes from the top shelf, but she said nothing.

A few minutes later, when she came out of the closet, she was dressed in a T-shirt and cutoffs, her wet hair now dripping on the bed.

"Ever heard of a towel?" I said as she slid up next to me.

"I think you're wrong," she said. "About Lionel. I think he probably just told you that stuff to deflect the question."

"Maybe," I said. "It's possible."

She slid up closer.

"Seriously," she said. "I know at least three women who have slept with him in the past year."

"Really?"

"Really," she said. She sat up then and wiped the water off her arm. "I kind of get the sense that Lionel is like that Quik Stop around the corner."

"How's that?"

"Oh, you know," she said, smiling, "always open for business."

Over the next few days I made a careful study of Lionel and what was going on with Caroline in the mornings, but nothing seemed unusual. She always arrived before Maya and I woke up and always left just as I was standing at the kitchen sink making us breakfast. She and Lionel would have a ceremonial cigarette before she left, rarely saying more than a few words to each other as they stood there, smoking, and then Lionel would give her a hug, pat her on the back, and leave.

Meanwhile, Maya rarely mentioned Lionel anymore. She was focused on a new set of paintings, all of them inspired by religious folk art she'd encountered in Oaxaca. These were perhaps the strongest paintings she'd done that summer, so good that she didn't even try to talk about them. One night, when we were sitting in the kitchen playing Scrabble and drinking beer, Maya still coming down from a long three-hour session in the studio, I told her that I hoped she wouldn't forget me when she was famous.

"Right," she said. She had never even had a gallery show outside of San Antonio at that point, but I could tell—and I think she could, too—that that was about to change.

"Lionel said that he'd be happy to put you in touch with some people," I said. "In New York. L.A. San Francisco."

"Why are you talking to Lionel about my work?"

"I'm not," I said. "He brought it up." I looked at her. "He's seen what you've been doing."

She looked away, and I could tell I'd hit a nerve. Maybe it was the superstitious thing.

"I don't want Lionel involved in my career," she said. "In any way. Okay?" She stared at me evenly.

"Okay," I said holding up my hands, and then I went into the other room to change the music.

When I came back out, Maya was standing at the kitchen sink, looking down at the courtyard, lost in thought. She seemed depressed. I came up behind her and put my arms around her stomach, and she squeezed my arm.

"This is a good time in our lives, isn't it?" she said.

"It is," I said and pulled her closer. "A very good time."

In the weeks that followed, our lives would take on a sort of tranquil simplicity. We'd wake each morning at the same time, share a quiet cup of coffee as we listened to the news, and then leave for work. In the evenings I'd return to find the kitchen empty and a note from Maya on the counter, usually with directions on how to heat up whatever it was she'd left for me in the freezer that night—chicken teriyaki, empanadas, lasagna. I think she left me these meals as a sort of peace offering, out of guilt, a way of saying I'm sorry for disappearing every night, but I never minded that she disappeared. She was in that rare space, as Lionel had said, and I was happy for her. I wanted her to work, and I never asked her to explain.

In the late evenings, when she returned from the studio, we'd lie in bed and listen to this UFO conspiracy show that always cracked us up, people calling in with eyewitness accounts, preposterous theories about the government's cover-ups, little-known facts about Area 51. Other times, we'd just lie there listening to the jazz station Maya liked or playing these books on tape that Lionel had lent us, classic novels and murder mysteries, short stories by Edgar Allan Poe. Maya liked her wine at night, and sometimes we'd roll a joint, if I had managed to track down some pot through one of my coworkers at the coffee shop, but mostly we'd just lie there, not talking, listening to the radio or tapes, a silent conversation passing between us.

By that point, Maya had stopped accepting any social invitations at all, and so had I. She had become very protective of her time, her space. I think she was aware that something special was happening and didn't want to ruin it. She wanted to keep the routine regular. Morning coffee, then work and studio time, followed by our late-night ritual of lying in bed and listening to the radio.

Meanwhile, Lionel had stopped coming out to the courtyard in the evenings, and Caroline had stopped showing up in the mornings, and so it often felt like it was just the two of us in this quiet back courtyard, overgrown with vines and flowering desert plants, succulents and salvias. I would have thought that I might have been lonely living this way, but I wasn't, even with Maya disappearing for four- or five-hour stretches at a time. I had my books, and I had my music, and I'd recently started writing letters to old friends, people I'd known in college but never saw anymore.

Once in a while I'd have a feeling that I was missing out on something or being left behind, but usually that feeling would pass. I'd get phone calls sometimes from my parents in Claremont, asking if I had figured out what I wanted to do for a career yet, had I received that book they'd sent on finding your inner drive, but I usually didn't let these things distract me. I was thirty-one and I liked my job. I didn't feel ashamed of my life, and as long as I was with Maya I felt that I was contributing in some small way to something larger than myself, to someone else's art, simply by being there. I was a part of her process, she'd told me one time, and I believed this.

Once she'd even told me that she didn't think that she'd be able to finish any of the paintings she was working on currently—she was now beginning to see them as a show—if I wasn't there.

She said this to me one night as we were sitting in the kitchen and lighting up our cigarettes. I'd put on some Nina Simone and Maya was jittery with excitement, having just finished the last four paintings in what she was calling a ten-painting series. She'd shown these paintings to Lionel earlier that week, she told me that evening, and he'd offered to make a phone call on her behalf to a gallery in San Francisco.

"I thought you didn't want him involved in your career," I said.

"Did I say that?"

"Many times."

It was early September now, but the evenings were still warm, and we had all of the windows open and the fans running full blast.

"Well, I guess I changed my mind then," she said.

"Any reason?"

"No." She shook her head. "It was just time. That's all."

And I knew what she meant: she'd finished the work she'd started at the beginning of the summer—she had seen it all the way through, this strange period of artistic output—and now it was over.

She stood up then and walked over to the sink and stood there with her cigarette.

"I thought you said he was a predator," I said after a moment, though I didn't know why I said this, why I couldn't drop it.

"Huh?"

"Lionel," I said. "You once called him a predator."

She pretended to ignore me.

"He's not a terrible person," she said, and then she dropped her cigarette in the sink and went into the bathroom to change.

The next morning when I woke, Maya was still asleep. I went over to the window and looked down at the courtyard and noticed Caroline, standing in a pair of cutoffs and a white T-shirt, smoking. Lionel wasn't there at first, but after a few minutes he appeared from the back of his house, clearly annoyed. It had been a few weeks since I'd seen Caroline around, and I wondered why. I asked Maya once, but she said she had no idea. *Probably lost interest,* she'd said, referring to Lionel. But that morning it was clear that Caroline was upset. I watched her as she waved her hands around, and then as she flicked her lit cigarette at Lionel's bare feet, causing him to jump. A moment later, she was walking away, disappearing down the small gravel path at the side of the house. Lionel stood there for a moment, then he looked around and headed back inside.

When Maya woke up, I didn't mention anything about what I'd seen, and that evening after work I didn't mention it either. I actually came home to find the apartment empty and no sign of Maya at all.

The lights in Lionel's studio were off; so were the lights in his house. I sent her a text but got no reply.

After a while, I decided to go down to the studio, just to check in person, to be sure, but the studio was empty, and all of Maya's paintings were covered with canvas tarps. I went around to the white worktable where Lionel often left out his work, and though the work he'd been doing lately was less provocative, mostly still lifes, that night I saw a nude, a series of them, actually, all of the same woman, all of them very similar in composition. The woman in the paintings was very vaguely rendered and impossible to discern or identify in any definitive way, though I was certain it wasn't Caroline, as the woman had dark hair—hair that was roughly the same length and color as Maya's, though it could have been anyone, really.

It's hard now to describe how I felt at that moment. Confused. Sad. Uncertain. I stared at the paintings for a long time, trying to suss out who it was, though of course it was impossible to tell. There was nothing definable there, no identifiable characteristics, and yet somehow I still felt certain it was her, that it was Maya. How do you know such things? I don't know that I can answer that, even now. All I know is that when I looked at those paintings, I knew.

When Maya returned later that night she was giddy with excitement and clearly drunk. She had gone out earlier with Lionel and some of his artist friends to celebrate the good news: the gallery owner that Lionel had put her in touch with in San Francisco, the one she'd sent some images of her work to, had called that morning to offer her a show. Just a three-week show, but even so, it was her first real show at a legitimate gallery outside of Texas. She claimed that she'd tried to call me so I could join them but that the reception at the restaurant was terrible. Then she'd tried to text me but her phone charge ran out. She held up her phone to show me it was dead.

I said nothing. She was so excited about the show I didn't have the heart to bring up Lionel's paintings or my suspicions about them. I don't know what I would have said to her anyway, or what I could have said if she had denied that the woman in the paintings was her. It's not like I could prove anything. So instead I just held her closely and congratulated her and then I poured us both a glass of wine and made a toast.

"So, when do you think the show will be?" I asked.

"No idea," she said. "It's still pretty up in the air. There's a lot of paperwork to sign, and stuff like that, you know—"

"But it's happening."

"It is," she said. "As far as I can tell."

I put down my glass and stared at her, and already there was that sense that she had left. Something in her eyes. It was maybe the only time in my life when I have felt that way in the presence of another person—that I was looking at someone who was already gone.

She walked up to me. "You know, maybe we can stay at your parents' when we go out there."

"Sure," I said, though I knew, as she must have known the moment she said it, that this would never come about.

It had been happening all summer, this gradual pulling away, but I hadn't felt it physically until that moment. There was a different energy in the room now, a different mood. Maya was looking forward, and I was somewhere in the background, on a distant train platform, watching.

"I still can't believe it," she said to me later that night, as we lay in bed. "I mean, did you ever think this would happen?"

"I did," I said.

"You did? Really?"

"Sure," I said. "I never had a doubt."

Over the next few months, Maya would travel out to San Francisco several times to meet with the gallery owner and talk about her work, and each time she came back more in love with the Bay Area and more certain that she wanted to move out there. She'd been to my parents' place in Claremont several times before, but somehow Southern California didn't resonate with her in the same way that the Bay Area did, especially San Francisco. She compared it to Europe, said there was just a lot more going on there, in terms of the art world. She'd apparently met other artists, other gallery owners.

I could see what was happening and understood, as I'd understood the moment she told me about her show, that I was powerless to stop it, that this no longer involved me. She had wanted to leave San Antonio for years, and now she finally had her chance.

I remember one night standing with her in the kitchen as she spoke on the phone to the gallery worker who was helping her with the transportation of her artwork. It was a complicated process for some reason, and when Maya got off the phone she looked exhausted, frustrated. I walked up beside her and put my arms around her, and I remember her standing there so stiffly, so rigidly, that I knew almost immediately that something was different. The next day over breakfast, she asked me if I had time to take a walk before work.

"A walk," I said. "Sure. What's up?"

But I already knew what was up. I could see it in her eyes. I knew that this was the talk we'd been avoiding for weeks.

"Let's just go for a walk," she said, and that was it. That was the end.

And though I remember us both crying on that walk, as we moved along the river a few blocks from our apartment, I knew I wasn't angry with her, just as I hadn't been angry with her when I found those watercolors in Lionel's studio. With any other girlfriend, I would have been, but for some reason I wasn't with Maya. That's just not how it was with us. She had already asked me several times to move out to the Bay Area with her, and each time I had told her I couldn't. Not because I didn't want to, but because I knew how it would end. Instead of being single in San Antonio, I would be single in California, and that wasn't something I wanted.

Later that night, as we were sitting in our apartment, talking about the logistics of when we would move out, what we'd tell Lionel, and so on, Maya disappeared for a minute and then came back with a small painting in her hands, an oil painting that she lay down before me on the table. The painting was of a still life from our apartment that summer, a glass of wine, the tiny black radio we kept above the kitchen sink, a pack of cigarettes, and a few of the succulents from the pot we kept on the windowsill.

She didn't say anything about the painting or why she was giving it to me. She just set it down on the table and then walked out of the room.

Later that night, as I lay in bed, Maya came into the room and lay down beside me. We still hadn't figured out what the sleeping arrangements would be like now. She rested her head on my chest, and I put my arms around her. In a year she would discover a small lump in a lymph node and her life would be forever changed, but at that moment she couldn't have been more vibrant, more alive. And later that night, after we'd had sex, I cried again, this time because I knew it had been the last time, and Maya had cried, too, perhaps for the same reason. The sex had been terrible, and we both laughed about this later on, as we stood in the kitchen doing the dishes.

After we finished, Maya sat down at the table for one last ciga-rette before bed, and that's when she brought up the issue of the triptych. She said that the gallery owner she'd been working with had wanted her to use it in the show, and she wanted to know how I felt about that. I told her that this would be fine, because I didn't know what else I could tell her. She nodded.

"But I want you to have this one," she said, handing me the still life. It was, I realized only then, a gorgeous painting.

"Why?" I said.

"Because," she said as she turned to leave the room, "it's my favorite."

In 2014, a few months before she died, Maya sent me an email with some photographs of her new house in Walnut Creek, just out-side of Berkeley, and her two children, four and six. She'd been in remission for about ten years at that point, and she looked great. She said that she'd been running about three or four miles a day, eating well. She said that she felt better than she had in many years. She made a comment about one of the photos she'd sent, the last one, in which she was dressed in what she called "mom clothes," standing next to her daughter outside her daughter's school. *Can you believe this is me?* she'd written. *Look at how normal I've become. All those years ago, who would have thought?*

I tried to remember her as she had been during that last sum-mer in San Antonio, her paint-speckled overalls, her hippie sandals, her long hair hanging down her back. Her hair now was short, her clothes conservative, expensive. I didn't know much about her hus-band, only that he had done well during the tech boom in the late nineties and was now semiretired. At the very end of the email Maya made a few references to our time together at Lionel's, which was something she almost never did. She said she often thought about those days, but that was all. I knew that she'd never made another painting after she moved to San Francisco, and though she never said why, I suspected it had something to do with her cancer diagnosis the year after she left, an experience that she said had changed her in such a fundamental way she couldn't even remember who she'd been before. She went through a bone marrow transplant and two rounds of chemo that year, and, when she came out on the other side of it, she wrote me an email in which she said, *I'm writing this to you from my email account but I am no longer me.*

I never asked her to explain what she meant by this, and she never did.

Over the years, we went through periods of writing to each other often, and periods when several months would pass, sometimes even a year, with no contact at all. During that entire time, she never mentioned her artwork or why she had stopped painting, and I didn't ask. It was simply another part of her life, I assumed. The life she had had with me was a different life than the life that she had now with her husband and children.

And though I don't find myself thinking about Maya as much as I used to, when I do, I usually think back to that night I discovered the watercolors in Lionel's studio, those nudes, and wonder, as I did that night, if they were her.

If they had been her: What was she thinking when she posed for him? Why did she do it? I try to imagine her coming home from work early and stopping by his studio, taking off her clothes as he sat there behind his small wooden easel. What had they talked about that afternoon while I was at the coffee shop, completely unaware? If the woman in the watercolors had in fact been her, what had she hoped to get from Lionel that he probably couldn't give her?

And what had she wanted from me? Was it the same thing she

wanted from Lionel? Maya and I slept together, side by side, for almost two years of our lives, and yet I wonder, even now, if I ever really knew her. Or if she ever really knew me.

Lionel Merritt died a few years before Maya, also of cancer, though I never saw him again after that fall when we moved out of the apartment above his garage. I did see Caroline again, though. This was a few years ago, at a fundraiser in the city for a local arts program. She was ten years older, of course, but looked practically the same. Still beautiful, still youthful, still tan. I waved to her across the room, but it was clear from the way she smiled at me tentatively, the way she turned away and then whispered something briefly to her friend, that she had no idea who I was.

Limes

I remember the first housewarming gift we received was a Mexican lime tree. It was given to us by our friend Lorena, who is a sculptor of some local renown, and it was delivered to us in a gorgeous ceramic pot that Lorena herself had made. *This thing will live forever,* she'd said to us the night she'd dropped it off. And she was right. That Mexican lime tree proved to be the most resilient of all of the plants and trees on our back deck, the only one to make it through that first frosty winter in San Antonio. By spring, we were using those limes to garnish our margaritas, and by summer Lorena was married again, her fifth husband and, she hoped, her last. *I love and I love and I love being in love,* she often said, *and I even like getting married. But somehow I just don't seem to like being married.* But that fifth one would stick, and for years afterward I would make a connection between that marriage and our lime tree. I'm not really sure why. I'm not a superstitious person, but I was about that tree. Winter after winter, I would water it and protect its leaves with burlap tarps. Somehow it seemed the most important thing in the world that it not die.

Cello

A few days after my forty-second birthday, my wife, Natalie, and I went to a lecture at the university where she teaches. The lecture was on the idea of the real self and whether or not such a thing as a real self exists. The lecturer, a young woman in her early thirties, who apparently teaches at the University of Texas, concluded that while no, such a thing as a real self does not exist, many people believe it does and therefore the concept of a real self is very powerful.

There was more to the lecture than that, of course, but that was the gist of it, and as we left the small auditorium where the lecture was held and headed back along the wooded pathway toward our car I could tell that Natalie was bothered by something. She had been invited to a small reception afterward—some sort of informal thing on the other side of campus—but had decided not to go. Instead she said that she just wanted to get home, pay the sitter, put the kids to bed, and have a drink. She looked worn out, like she hadn't slept in several days, and the whole way home she looked out the window absently, tapping her fingers along the dashboard or, alternately, resting her hands in her lap. I tried my best not to look at her hands—it had become a bad habit lately—but couldn't help myself. I noticed that the right one was fine, but that the left was trembling slightly, though not as badly as it had been that morning.

At a stoplight, I asked her how she was feeling. She shrugged. "About the same. Mostly just tired."

I nodded and looked out the window at the quiet, wooded streets of our neighborhood, a small, secluded neighborhood near campus where we have lived for almost seven years now, a neighborhood that reminds me so much of the Connecticut neighborhood I grew up in that I often forget we live in Texas.

"You know," she said after a moment, "no one at the lecture even looked at me."

"You mean from the department?"

"Yeah."

"I think you're probably just imagining that," I said and reached over and touched her hand.

"No, David," she said and looked out the window. "I really don't think I am." She sighed and straightened her dress. "You know, I can take a lot of things, but pity—that's one thing I can't take."

"I don't think anyone's pitying you," I said, and reached over again for her hand. "Besides, what if they are? Let them. What does it matter, anyway?"

"Well, you're not the one who has to work with them," she said, and then she looked out the window again. "You're not the one who has to deal with their stares."

. . .

At home I paid the sitter while Natalie went into the bedroom and undressed. The kids were already in bed—we have a daughter, Eryn, and a son, Finn, two and five respectively—and after I walked the sitter to the door I went into their bedroom to check on them. They'd been sharing a bedroom lately, ever since Eryn had graduated from her crib, and so far it had worked out pretty well. Finn seemed to respect the fact that Eryn was still a toddler and would occasionally wake up and cry, and Eryn seemed to accept the fact that she had left the familiar comfort of her parents' bedroom and was now sleeping on her own. For two siblings born so close together, they were amazingly compatible with each other, even sweet at times. I knew that this probably wouldn't last, but for now, at least, it was working.

That night I stood there for a while in the dim light of their room, watching them sleep, wondering if I should wake them and let them know that we were home. They both looked so angelic at that moment, so at peace, so different from how they normally looked during the day. On the other side of the house, I could hear the shower going on—a sign that Natalie was probably especially tired tonight—so after a while I turned off the light and then headed back toward the kitchen in search of the wine.

This had become a bit of a nightly ritual lately, the drinking of wine before bed, or after dinner, a ritual that we'd picked up shortly after Natalie discovered that a glass or two each night seemed to relax her nerves and ease her tremors, and though it was a short-lived relief, rarely lasting longer than half an hour, it had begun to make her evenings manageable. That night I pulled out several bottles, unsure of what she might be in the mood for, and then I set out the wineglasses, the cheese, a bowl of olives. I dimmed the lights and searched through the drawers for a corkscrew. Outside the window above the kitchen sink, I could hear the distant hiss of our neighbors' sprinkler system, and across the lawn that separated our two houses

I could see our neighbors' daughter, a teenager, sitting on their back deck passing a joint back and forth with a friend.

It was early evening now, a faint breeze moving through the trees at the far end of our yard, the last light of the day fading. I stood at the sink for a while longer, watching the sun descend beyond the loquat trees and the tool shed and the small studio in the back. I heard the shower go off on the other side of the house, and then a few minutes later I heard some music go on, not classical music, the music that Natalie had been trained in and devoted her life to, the music that had filled every apartment and every house we'd ever lived in, but Bessie Smith, a newfound love, a rich and soulful presence in our lives these days. I uncorked the wine, filled two glasses, making sure to fill Natalie's only halfway—any higher than that and she tended to shake it out—and then I sat down at the island in the middle of the room and waited.

After a while Natalie emerged in her bathrobe, her hair combed back from her face, her arms crossed, and as she walked across the living room and into the kitchen I stood up to embrace her. She came to me and buried her head in my chest, and for a moment I just held her, rubbing her back and then her shoulder, the sore one, the one that she had begun to call the bane of her existence.

"Still sore?" I asked as she pulled away and sat down on a stool at the island.

"Every time I play on the A-string," she said and sighed. "This morning I thought I was making progress, you know, it felt okay, but ever since lunch it's been killing me."

In the past few weeks, Natalie has been experimenting with the positioning of her cello, extending the endpin so that she has the cello at a lower angle and slightly to the right, and she's also been using a heavier bow to lessen the tremor, and trying to control it by tensing up her right arm. But all these changes have resulted in other problems, most significantly a sharp throbbing in her right shoulder whenever she plays for longer than half an hour.

"But I don't want to talk about any of that tonight," she said, putting down her glass.

"Okay," I said. "What do you want to talk about?"

"Anything else," she said and smiled.

I walked over to the cabinet and pulled out some bread. "I talked to Frances today," I said. "She said that she'd like to see you this week."

"Did you tell her I was worse?"

"No," I said. "Because I'm not convinced that you *are* worse. From what I can tell, it seems to ebb and flow, right?"

She stared at me. "It's *my* body, David, and I'm telling you it's worse." She walked over to the window and looked out again at the neighbor girl and her friend on their back deck, smoking. She seemed to consider them for a moment, and then turned away.

"By the way, did I mention that Finn's begun to notice?"

"Notice what?"

"The way I hold my fork now. My handwriting. The fact that I can't put pigtails in Eryn's hair."

"*I* can't put pigtails in Eryn's hair," I said.

She looked at me and then took another sip of wine. "You know, at a certain point we're going to have to talk about this, David."

"About what?"

"About the children."

"The children are going to be fine," I said. "We're all going to be fine."

"David, there might be a time when you're having to take care of everything around here, and we're going to have to talk about what that's going to look like."

"We'll figure it out when it happens," I said. "*If* it happens."

"There's no *if*," she said.

"You don't know that."

"Yes," she said, "I do."

Many people go through life and they never need to know what a term like *deep brain stimulation* means. For a long time I was one of those people, and so was Natalie, and then one night, as we were coming home from a party, driving along a quiet street near campus, Natalie held up her pinky and asked me if I noticed anything strange about it, anything unusual, and though I was driving I could see that it was shaking slightly, a small tremor. It was barely noticeable.

A few days later, over dinner, she told me she'd noticed that her down-bows had been shaking quite a lot over the past few weeks, especially on the down-bows in the middle of the bow. And the double-stops in the middle of the bow were even worse. I suggested that she make an appointment with our family doctor, but she'd already made an appointment by then to see a specialist, a neurologist. She knew. She would tell me this weeks later, as we were standing in line at a restaurant, that at the moment we were having that conversation, she already knew.

The neurologist she saw ran a series of tests on her but felt it was too early to make an official diagnosis. He mentioned that one possibility was Parkinson's, of course, but he felt it was more likely essential tremor, a condition that's typically less severe and not always progressive, but still life-altering, especially for someone like Natalie, whose livelihood depends on her hands. He told her that in some cases the tremor might get worse over time, but in others it stayed the same, or barely changed, and in some rare cases it even got better. At this point the tremor was only in Natalie's hands, which was good, and it was mainly in her right hand. What he wanted to do right now was monitor it. Monitor it and wait.

For a few days after that Natalie went into a bit of depression, anticipating the worst. She talked a lot about her career and what this was going to mean for her, not just as a performer but also as a newly tenured professor in the Department of Music. She'd recently been appointed chair of the string area. She taught courses on music theory and gave weekly lessons to several students in the department, not to mention her commitment to the university's string quartet and all her other performance obligations, some of which required her to travel great distances. Her doctor had warned her that any type of stress in her life, whether physical or emotional, could potentially set off her tremors and that she needed to cut down on her commitments considerably if she wanted to continue to play the cello. He'd told her this at her second appointment, later that week. He also prescribed beta blockers for her performances and recommended a physical therapist in our area who specialized in ET, and then he gave her a pamphlet with some surgical options, including deep brain stimulation.

Natalie came home from that appointment in a bit of a daze. She told me a little about what the doctor had told her, though not everything, and then she said that she needed to be alone. I watched her walk out to the studio in our backyard that her brother Trent built for her last year. Trent is an architect at a fairly prestigious firm up in Austin, and he and some of his colleagues designed this studio for Natalie's fortieth birthday last June. Natalie's father paid for it, but I could tell that for Trent it was a labor of love. The walls of the studio are made entirely of glass, and though the studio itself is fairly small, only twenty feet by twenty feet, at night, when Natalie is playing out there, it often resembles a large glass cube glowing in the middle of our back lawn.

That night Natalie didn't take her cello along with her, though. She walked out to the studio by herself and sat down on a small chair in the middle of the room. The walls of the studio are soundproof, but I could tell that she was listening to music. I could tell by the way she was just sitting there in the middle of the glass-walled room with her eyes shut, leaning back in her chair, a glass of wine on the floor beside her.

When she came in a few hours later, she said nothing. She just went to bed, and when she woke up the next day, she seemed possessed by a newfound optimism and determination. She wouldn't be stepping down from her position as chair of the string area, she said; she wouldn't be relinquishing her responsibilities as a professor; and she wouldn't be walking away from the string quartet. She'd take the beta blockers, as the doctor suggested, she'd start physical therapy, she'd watch her diet, try to exercise more, keep a healthier outlook on things. She'd do all the things the doctor and the support forums she visited online suggested. It was going to be a tough road, yes—potentially a very tough road—but she wasn't going to let the condition define her.

I watched her with a kind of stunned amazement as she did all the things she said she was going to do, as she continued to teach her classes and lead her solo lessons, as she continued to practice with the university's string quartet, as she told her colleagues without embarrassment or fear what was happening to her, as she even joked with some of our friends about what our lives were going to be like in the future, about how inventive we'd have to be about sex or about how terrible she was going to look when I was the one doing her makeup. This went on for about two or three months, I guess—this period of optimism—and then one day, maybe about three or four weeks ago, I came home and found her lying in bed, complaining of an intense dizziness that she couldn't make stop. She was in tears and asked me to call the music department and explain that she wouldn't be coming in. I could tell that she was scared.

"I think we need to go to the hospital," I said.

"No," she said. "We don't. It's happened before. It'll pass."

"Let me know what I can do."

"Just turn off the lights," she said. "And close the door, and when you go to get the kids later on just tell them I'm sick or something."

I turned off the lights, as she'd asked, and then stood for a moment in the doorway, watching her. She had her eyes closed, and in the darkness I could see her chest moving up and down slowly. I couldn't tell if she knew I was there, but after a moment she turned and looked up at me, just briefly, and sighed.

"I'm sorry, David," she said.

"For what?"

But she didn't answer. She just closed her eyes and turned away.

Since that evening, she hasn't wanted to talk about her classes or the string quartet or her future as a performer; she's only wanted to talk about the children and our future and what that's going to look like, and she's wanted to talk about it with an intensity and an urgency that worries me. I try to remind her about what the doctor has told us—that at this point it's way too early to know anything specific, and that though, yes, the dizziness is troubling, in isolation it doesn't necessarily mean anything. Still, I can tell that these recent changes to her body have worried her. A few days ago she canceled her performance with the university's string quartet. They were doing several pieces by Erwin Schulhoff and the famous "Kreutzer

Sonata" by Leoš Janáček, one of Natalie's favorites, and I knew it devastated her. The night she told me this I was in the kitchen making Eryn's dinner. Finn was at a neighbor's house, playing with one of their sons, and had he been there she probably wouldn't have cried, but that night she did. That night she lost it. It was the first time she'd wept since the day she was diagnosed.

Later that night, as we were lying in bed, I tried to get her to talk to me about what had happened with the string quartet. These are people we've known for many years, close friends we've vacationed with, had over for dinner countless times. I knew that there was more to the story than what she was telling me, but she wouldn't elaborate. I told her I found it hard to believe that they would've just let her walk away like that, but she said nothing.

The following day I called Frances, Natalie's closest friend and the lead violinist in the string quartet, and asked her what had happened. I've known Frances for almost seven years and admire her very much. I knew that she'd tell me the truth. But Frances was cagey at first, evasive, and then finally, after a little prodding, she admitted that Natalie had been difficult lately—"querulous" was the word she used. She'd been having trouble keeping up with the rest of the group, Frances said, and they'd had to talk to her about the possibility of stepping down for a while, just till she had a better sense of what was going on with her body and how she might control it. They'd talked about this openly, as a group, and Natalie had apparently sat there for a long time listening, not saying a word. Finally, after they'd all given their opinion, she'd stood up, packed up her cello, and left. They all felt terrible for her, Frances said, they couldn't even begin to imagine, but they had to move forward as well. Frances's voice kept breaking as she was telling me this, and she kept apologizing, but I told her not to worry about it, that I completely understood.

"You know, if she ever just wants to play," Frances said at the end, "I'm sure I could talk to the others—" But I stopped her before she could finish.

That night I tried to bring it up with Natalie again, but she said that she was over it, that she didn't want to think about the string quartet anymore, and that she was already moving on. She accused me of being sentimental, of being in some type of denial. She said I needed to get a clearer perspective on things.

Later that night I called Frances again and asked her if there was any chance that Natalie could rejoin the quartet if her symptoms improved and if she apologized to the others, but I don't know why I did this. I already knew the answer.

"We've already found a replacement," Frances said, softly. "I'm sorry, David."

"Who?"

"Does it really matter?"

"Is it Eric Janowitz?" I said. Eric was Natalie's star student for several years, her protégé, before he graduated and joined the faculty himself as an adjunct.

Frances didn't answer. Instead, she said, "How are you both doing, David? Everyone here is so worried. Not just about Natalie, but about you, too. We want to help out in any way we can."

I thanked her for her concern and then told her we were fine, and though I felt a touch annoyed—after all, Natalie had gone to bat for Frances many times (in department meetings, with the other members of the group)—I said nothing else. I told her we'd be in touch.

Natalie was back at the window now, the window above the sink, staring out at the neighbor girl and her friend. It was almost dark.

"Do you think they're smoking a joint?" she said.

"No," I said. "I think it's just a cigarette."

She shook her head. "When did she turn into such a teenager? Do you remember what she was like when we first moved in?"

"A kid," I said. "But that was seven years ago."

She shook her head again and sipped her wine, and I knew where her mind was going now: to our own children and what it would be like when they were teenagers, especially if her symptoms progressed, especially if she was worse off then than she was now. She had recently shown me some videos on the internet, the worst-case scenarios, as she called them. She said that she wanted me to be prepared for the worst, to know what our lives might look like if she had Parkinson's or something worse. After the second video, I made her stop. I told her that I wouldn't be watching these videos anymore. Now I could see that her mind was returning there, so I tried to steer the conversation back to Frances and her ongoing efforts to reach out to her. I reminded her that Frances had called the house at least a dozen times that week, maybe more.

Natalie rolled her eyes and put down her glass.

"You know, apparently it's Eric Janowitz," she said. "My replacement."

"Are you surprised?"

"No. But I know he'll never step down. Even if my symptoms improve."

"You don't know that."

"Yes, I do," she said. "He's too ambitious."

"Well, there are other quartets."

"Not for me."

"What about solo stuff? You could travel again."

"David." She stared at me. "I can barely hold a fork."

She nodded for me to fill up her empty glass again, which I did. It was her third of the night.

"I'm cutting you off after this," I said, sliding the glass back to her. She ignored this and sat down on her stool.

"I keep thinking about what that woman at the lecture was saying, you know, about how our choices and actions are judged in terms of their relationship to the true self and how those acts that are congruent with one's true self are deemed valuable. But what about when you are no longer in control of your choices and actions? What about when you're no longer in control of your own body?"

She looked at me.

Earlier that night, toward the end of the lecture, the woman who was lecturing had said that she wanted to conduct a little experiment just to prove a point.

She had her teaching assistants pass out scraps of white paper and small pencils and then asked everyone in the audience to write down words in two columns—one column for words that best described their "true" self, the other for words that best described their "actual" self. Natalie had had trouble holding the tiny pencil and eventually gave up, but not before I'd caught a glimpse of a few of the words she'd written down: *mother, perfectionist, vessel, abandoner, cripple, cellist, ghost.* I didn't know what to make of these words or what column she intended to include them in. It was painful to read them. I leaned over to say something to her, but before I could she crumpled up the paper. Now I wondered what those words had meant, why she'd written them. I could no longer remember what the point of the experiment had been.

"I mean, what happens to my true self when my body is no longer my own?" she continued. "What happens when I can no longer dress myself? When I can no longer comb my own hair?"

"I think you've had enough wine," I said.

"I'm asking you something very serious here, David, and you're not listening to me."

"I am," I said and walked over to her. "You're scared. It's understandable. I'm scared, too."

"But that's just the thing," she said, sipping her wine. "I'm not scared at all."

On the night I met Natalie, our junior year in college, she was performing a cello concerto by Dmitri Shostakovich as part of the spring concert series. She was the only student in the show with a solo performance, and I'd find out later on that this was because she was the best cellist to pass through Oberlin College in the past ten years. When people spoke about her, they used words like *prodigy* and *virtuoso* without exaggeration.

Later on that night, I was introduced to her backstage by a mutual friend, a woman whose name I no longer recall, and we ended up going to a keg party at some dorm on the other side of campus along with seven or eight other students from the college's orchestra. After the party we walked along the quiet streets on the east edge of campus as we made our way back to her dorm by the river just as the sun was coming up.

But before all of that I remember watching her on the stage and being aware, though I knew nothing about music, that I was in the presence of greatness. That I was observing a singular and remarkable talent. I remember watching the way her bow moved, so fluidly, as if it were an extension of her body, a part of her arm, and the way she closed her eyes at certain points in the performance and seemed to disappear within herself, the way her breathing sped up and then slowed down as the tempo increased or fell off, and the way she seemed to brighten at certain moments, as if awakened from a dream or a trance. It was all very intimate and hypnotic and I found it hard to look away from her, hard not to stare at her, even as the performance was ending. I remember how the lights came on and everyone in the audience stood up and clapped. I remember how they all kept standing there, clapping their hands, for several minutes.

This was what I was thinking about later on that night, as I stood in our backyard in the dark, watching Natalie through the glass walls of her studio.

Earlier, after she'd checked on the kids, after we'd both finished off a second bottle, she'd gone into the bedroom to look for her cello. I thought she'd only want to check the bridge, to check if it was slanting—this had been an issue lately—but a few minutes later she came out with the entire case, saying that she felt like playing. I reminded her that it was almost ten o'clock and that the doctor had recommended she start going to bed earlier, but she ignored this and went into the kitchen for more wine.

A moment later, I watched her walk out to the studio in the backyard, watched her as she moved through the darkness with her cello under one arm, the bottle of wine in the other. I waited until I saw the lights go on in the studio, the glass-walled cube suddenly aglow, and then I headed out to the backyard to watch.

That night Natalie didn't open up her cello case, though. Instead she just set it down in the corner of the room and then she sat down on the one small chair in the middle and turned on the stereo system connected to her iPod. I watched the equalizer lights turn on, and then I saw Natalie lean her head back and close her eyes, just as she had that other night, the bottle of wine on the floor beside her.

I thought about the children asleep in their rooms and how sad it would be if they never got to see their mother play, really play, in the way I had, in the way she had that first night I met her, in the way she had so many times in this very studio, late at night, while they were asleep in their rooms. They might have memories of her playing now, or in the past, but they would be distant memories, vague and incomplete. They wouldn't be memories like this. I thought about Natalie's symptoms lately—her dizziness and her loss of balance—both things that we knew to be connected to Parkinson's and that the doctor had admitted were "troubling." He had asked her to come in for some more tests earlier that week—more blood tests and an MRI—and now we were waiting, waiting as it seemed we had been for many months, floating in this liminal space, not knowing what the future might hold, and yet fearing every outcome, feeling in our private moments what we always seemed to feel now: the utter frailty of our own bodies, how suddenly and inexplicably they might fail us.

I moved in a little closer to the studio then, though not so close that Natalie could see me. I could feel the cool earth beneath my bare feet, a gentle breeze at my back. It was very dark out, dark except for the intense, glowing light from the studio. I moved in closer. I watched Natalie lean her head forward, relax her shoulders. I wondered what might happen if I waved to her or called out her name. I wondered if she might see me, if she might come to the door, just this once, and let me in.

Rhinebeck

For the past few years, my daily routine has been pretty much the same: I wake up around six, make myself a large pot of coffee, read the morning paper, go for a run, shower and shave, then work on my freelance assignments until about five. After that, I open a bottle of wine, answer emails for about an hour, then head over to Fontaine, where I always sit at the same place at the wine bar. Rebecca is almost always there, standing behind the bar, and we usually share a couple of glasses of wine and then Colette, or one of the other waitresses, will begin to bring me things—little sample plates of whatever they're serving that night—and David or one of the other chefs will come out from time to time to check on me and ask me what I think. "Delicious," I'll always say, "even better than last night." And they'll always smile and pat me on the back and tell me I'm lying, but I never am.

The food they make there is consistently great. It's one of the few things in my life I can rely on.

I've known the owners of Fontaine, David and Rebecca, for almost twenty years now. They're my oldest and closest friends and the reason I live here in Rhinebeck. We all went to college together down the road in Poughkeepsie, spent a couple of wild and unproductive years in New York, and then eventually moved up here to open Fontaine—or rather, they moved up here to open Fontaine, and I came along for the ride.

My initial plan was to stay only a couple of months, to help them out until they got the restaurant off the ground, but somehow those couple of months turned into a couple of years and those couple of years turned into twenty. When I think about it too much, which I try not to, it frightens me sometimes: just how quickly time can pass.

On a typical night, I'll stick around the restaurant until the evening service has ended; then I'll hang out for a while with the kitchen staff and waitresses, listening to them as they swap stories about the customers and drink wine and eat whatever's left over. From time to time, David will come out to join us, or Rebecca will stop by with a bottle of wine she's been considering for the menu, and we'll all take a sip and give her our opinions, and then she'll disappear for a while, only to appear a half hour later with something else: another bottle of wine, a plate of cheeses, a pluot tart. At some point, the kitchen staff will head outside to smoke, and the waitresses will start to text their boyfriends, and I'll be left there by myself in this dim-lit room, watching the candles flicker, the snow outside the window, swirling in slow motions.

Back in the early days, back when the restaurant was just starting out, I used to help them from time to time in the kitchen. It wasn't a regular thing and I wasn't paid for my time, but I still enjoyed it. Mostly what I did was a lot of prep work, something that David had schooled me in back in New York, back when he was still holding out hope that I'd follow him and Rebecca on their restaurant venture. I actually considered it for a while. I enjoyed the simple pleasure of chopping up vegetables for a salad or stirring a reduction or making a sauce. I liked the mindlessness of it, and the camaraderie in the kitchen, the arguments over which music to play or who was going to win the annual football pool. And I liked being around the two of them, too, watching them work together as a team, which was so seamless and organic you'd think they were two parts of the same person. But, in the end, I couldn't stomach the stress of it, the way the tension would build up on a really busy night or the way the cooks would turn on each other over the simplest thing: a missed order, an overcooked *crème brûlée*, a spoiled soup. By the end of the night I'd usually be so keyed up from all the stress that I'd have to smoke half a pack of cigarettes just to get to the point where I was ready to come back to the world and talk to people again.

These days I mostly stick around the front of the house with Rebecca. I like listening to her as she talks about her plans to remodel their home or as she gossips about the regulars who stop by the restaurant night after night. Sometimes, after she's had a little too much wine to drink, she'll grow expansive, talking at length about her various philosophies or cautioning me about the various problems in my life. She seems to think I'm depressed or, rather, that I'm missing out on something. I try to tell her that I'm not, that I enjoy my life the way it is, that I don't mind not having a girlfriend, or a regular job, or a house of my own. I've lived this way for almost twenty years, I tell her, and I'm not about to change. But still, she worries. She worries about me growing old alone, worries about what will happen to me after they leave in a couple of years, which has been their plan for the past six months: to sell Fontaine and move down to Texas and open up another restaurant in Austin. They've had similar plans in the past—once to open up a restaurant in New York, another time to move to Belize—but none of these plans have ever actually materialized, which is why I'm not that worried. But still, Rebecca presses me.

"I mean, what's going to happen to you?" she said to me the other night, as we were sitting over drinks. "What will you do?"

"I'll be fine," I said.

"Do you think you'll stay here?"

"In Rhinebeck?" I said. "Maybe." I looked at her. "Maybe I'll come along to Austin."

Outside the front window I could see the empty streets of Rhinebeck, covered in snow. The restaurant and shop windows were aglow from within, a warm light spilling out onto the sidewalk, fresh flakes floating down from the sky.

She looked at me evenly. "You hate Texas," she said.

"I could learn to love it," I said and winked.

"You're not taking this seriously."

"I am," I said. "I just don't see the point in worrying about something that hasn't happened yet."

"Because you don't believe it will."

"I didn't say that."

"No," she said, "but I can tell." She turned to me then and squeezed my hand. "You need to find something solid, Richard."

"What do you mean, something solid?"

"I mean, you need to find something solid in your life."

. . .

When I first met the two of them, back in college, we were all working together in the campus library's film department. Our job was to screen various films at night for the evening film classes and to keep the library's catalogue well stocked and organized. It was a pretty easy job and one that lent itself to many cigarette breaks.

David and Rebecca weren't a couple at first, but by the end of the fall semester, I'd begun to notice them showing up at each other's shifts, or sometimes sharing shifts, and then one night over the winter break I remember David showing up at my room in a drunken stupor, nearly in tears because he'd heard that Rebecca was getting back together with her old boyfriend. I'd asked him if he'd ever told her how he felt about her and he admitted he hadn't, that he'd always been too afraid to bring it up. So I'd taken him to a coffee shop near campus and sobered him up, and then I walked him back to Rebecca's dorm and waited outside for almost an hour, ready to console him if things didn't work out, but of course they did, and after a while, I saw the light go off in Rebecca's window and headed back home.

After college, we all moved down to the city for a while and we saw each other most weekends and often took trips together out to the Hamptons or up to small towns along the Hudson, like Rhinebeck or Newburgh. I'd found a job working as an assistant for a fairly prominent art magazine and David and Rebecca had started waiting tables and then cooking in various restaurants on the Upper East Side. David actually developed a bit of a talent for cooking and eventually got promoted to head chef at a somewhat small, but well-respected French restaurant near their apartment, or the apartment they shared, on Eighty-Sixth Street. By then, though, his interests had shifted to opening his own place and to cooking the type of food he wanted to cook, and on top of that, I think they were both starting to feel a little burnt out on New York. Burnt out on the lifestyle, the cost of living. They wanted something quieter and simpler and cheaper. We went back to campus for our five-year reunion, and something seemed to happen that weekend. I don't know what it was, only that I went home on the train that Sunday, and David and Rebecca stayed on. They went up to Rhinebeck, and the next time I saw them they had already put down a down payment on the building that would later become Fontaine. The night they told me this we were all sitting around a small table at the most amazing Japanese restaurant on Thirty-Sixth Street, eating noodles, and I remember David looking up at me then with his mouth full of noodles and smiling. "This," he said, wiping his mouth with a napkin, then slurping up the last of the noodles. "This," he said, "I will miss."

In the end, it only took me about a month to move up there myself. I don't think they really expected me to stay in Manhattan. I'd already quit my job at the art magazine by then and had already begun to freelance, and the rent on my apartment had just been raised. There wasn't a whole lot keeping me down in the city anymore. Besides, they had started to put the hard sell on me the moment they told me.

"If you don't move up here," Rebecca had said that first time I visited them, "you realize we're going to kill each other, don't you?"

"He'll move up here," David had said, smiling. "He just doesn't realize it yet."

I told them I couldn't, that I'd feel like I was following them, that it would be too strange, but of course I'd already decided by then that I would, had already told my landlord and everything.

· · ·

On the day that I actually moved up, I remember the two of them driving me all around town. This would have been in the early fall of that year, and I remember that the leaves on the trees had just changed and that the air was just getting brisk and that everything around us was quiet and still, and I remember at one point David pulling over on the side of the road at this little farmers market and buying all of these autumnal vegetables and fruits—aubergine and cauliflower and sweet corn and pears, pumpkins and apples and chicory and squash. We went home that night and David cooked us the most amazing meal—I wish I could remember now what it was—and the three of us just sat there stuffing ourselves in their tiny makeshift kitchen, and then afterward, we all lay down on the floor of their apartment—they still hadn't bought a house yet—and passed a joint back and forth and listened to Leonard Cohen and talked about our lives, and I remember David turning to me at one point and asking me if I thought I could get used to this, and I remember telling him I could.

"I mean, in a permanent way," he said.

"I know," I said. "I mean that, too."

"You do?" he said. "So you think you'll stay on then?"

"I think I'm thinking about it," I said.

"Good," he said, and squeezed my hand tightly. "I'm glad."

Years later, I'd remember this night very vividly for some reason, the way we all sat outside on their back deck afterward, huddled under blankets in the cold, the lights of the distant farmhouses glowing, the smell of leaves burning, the bottle of wine we passed back and forth. A few weeks later David would admit to me that that night had basically saved them, that a few days earlier Rebecca had suffered a miscarriage and that he'd worried she might move back to New York permanently, that she'd seemed inconsolable. He'd embraced me then and thanked me, though I didn't know why. I didn't know what I'd done.

He told me that he was so glad I'd decided to move up here, and I told him not to worry too much about what had happened, that it happened to lots of couples, that it had happened to my own mother twice before she'd had me, and at the time I honestly believed that they'd eventually try again, but as far as I could tell they never did. Nor did they ever talk about it much, which always seemed sad to me, sad only because they would have been such great parents and that would have been the perfect time to do it, back when the restaurant was just starting up and they both had so much free time.

Years later, when I'd ask David about it, he'd claim that Fontaine was their baby, or other times, when he was being facetious, that I was. He'd say that the staff at the restaurant was like family to them, that he couldn't imagine wanting more. But when I'd ask Rebecca the same thing, when I'd bring up the topic of kids, she'd grow distant and removed. She'd get evasive or change the subject or she'd turn the question back on me.

"I mean, don't *you* ever think about it?" she'd say. "Isn't it something *you* want?"

"Well, to have children would necessitate having a wife first, or at least a girlfriend."

"Which you could have in a second if you wanted one."

"Right," I'd say, "and that's the key, isn't it? If I wanted one."

For years, Rebecca has been trying to set me up with various women at the restaurant. She used to do this a lot more when I was younger and closer in age to most of the staff. I think she felt a kind of maternal obligation to find me a mate or at least someone else to spend time with. Once or twice these little set-ups of hers actually worked out, and I'd end up dating the woman for a month or two, or sometimes longer, but in the end none of these relationships ever actually materialized into something bigger. There was never that spark, which was probably my fault, or if there was a spark, or a semblance of a spark, I'd always find a way to squash it out.

The latest person Rebecca tried to set me up with was their hostess, Rochelle. I'd known Rochelle for almost two years and would have probably asked her out a long time ago had she not had a boyfriend in New York. A few months ago, though, Rebecca informed me that Rochelle and her boyfriend had broken up, and then the next thing I knew we were all having dinner together at Rebecca and David's house, and then Rochelle and I were going out on a few dates, all of which went well, and talking about plans for the summer, how we might rent a house together out on the Cape for a couple weeks in July, and so forth.

It all seemed to be going pretty fast, though, and maybe that's why I started to pull back. I don't know. After a while, it just began to feel like all of the other relationships I'd had recently. There wasn't that closeness there, that trust. David says it isn't fair of me to always compare the women I date to the relationship he has with Rebecca or to the relationship the three of us have, that nothing can really compete with that, and that, besides, the three of us have at least twenty years of history between us. But I try to tell him that it doesn't have anything to do with that. It doesn't have anything to do with history at all. It's about closeness, I tell him. It's about that thing that's either there or it's not.

I'd tried to explain the same thing to Rochelle, too, on the night we broke up, but I could tell she didn't want to hear it. We were sitting in her car, parked outside my apartment late at night, the heat running, and I remember looking at her face as she stared out the window. Finally, after I finished, she said that the problem with me was that I didn't really want to be in a relationship, I only pretended I did.

"You're a person who avoids intimacy," she said to me later on, as we stood outside my apartment in the rain. "I think there's a name for that."

"A recluse?"

"No," she said, and smiled. "The word I was thinking of wasn't that nice."

It must have been sometime in late August, late August or early September, that David first told me about the Austin thing. We were sitting out on his back deck, enjoying these wonderful cigars that one of his cousins had sent him, and he just kind of mentioned it casually, how he'd been looking into some spaces in the downtown area, and how they were thinking about a two-year plan at this point, two or three years, depending. He was speaking kind of quietly and buffering everything he said with caveats, which is what he does whenever he's worried he might be offending me or hurting my feelings. I didn't really know what to make of it, honestly. I asked him if he was serious and he said that he was, kind of. He said that Rebecca had always wanted to go back there—she'd grown up in San Marcos—and that it was important for her to be closer to her parents now that they were getting older. Also, he said, the food scene was booming down there, so there was that. Still, he added at the end, at this point, it was all just speculation, conjecture. He just thought I should know.

I nodded and sipped on the beer I was drinking. It was a beautiful summer evening, quiet and cool, with a light breeze, the sun descending beyond the trees at the far end of their yard. David had that look on his face that he used to get back in the early days of his marriage, back when he used to confide in me about his problems with Rebecca, a kind of guilty look.

I smiled at him. "Of all the places," I said. "I would have never guessed Texas."

"Yeah." He shrugged. "Well, you know, Rebecca's family and all. It's something we've talked about for a while."

I nodded again.

"But, like I said, it's really just speculation at this point—kind of a pipe dream, honestly."

"Well, Fontaine was once, too."

"What?"

"A pipe dream."

"Yeah," he said, and smiled in a sort of distant, distracted way. "But that was different."

"Why?"

"I don't know," he said. "I guess because we were younger then, you know? We're not so young anymore, Rich."

He said this as if he was trying to tell me something he didn't think I knew, as if he was edifying me, and there was something almost deliberate about it. I put down my beer, but before I could say anything else, Rebecca appeared in the doorway behind us, framed in the light from the kitchen, holding a bottle of wine and a fresh pack of cigarettes, and we moved on to something else, another topic, and didn't mention it again that night.

Back in those early days in Rhinebeck, back when we were all just figuring stuff out and nothing was permanent or settled yet, we used to go into the city all the time. It was like none of us had fully accepted that it was over yet, that we'd left. We'd hop on the train on a Friday afternoon, make hotel reservations on the ride down, and then spend the night hitting all of our favorite bars and restaurants, staying up till four or five in the morning, just like we used to back in college. Rebecca loved it the most, I think. She was the one who'd been resistant to the idea of moving up here in the first place, the one who'd cried the moment they finally had to drop off the keys to their rent-controlled apartment.

She'd drink and rage all night, try to drag us to clubs that were far too young for us, beg us to go dancing with her. Just for an hour, she'd say. And sometimes we'd indulge her because it was more fun to watch Rebecca rage than it was to rage ourselves. She was still holding on back then, still trying to believe that nothing had changed, and for years afterward you'd sometimes see it in her eyes, tiny glimpses of that other self, that other self that used to fade the moment we stepped back onto the train to Rhinebeck, that seemed to grow duller and more distant with each passing town.

These days we almost never go into the city anymore, maybe once or twice a year to see a show or visit old friends, but back then there was this sense—and I realize now, it was probably just me—but there was this sense back then that we'd reached a kind of pinnacle in our youth, not that we were young anymore, just that we were still able to fake it, to slip back into those younger selves and be the people we were back in college. It was a trick, a game of make-believe, and we didn't do it often, but just enough to remind ourselves that we could.

And then one day it suddenly stopped. I'm not really sure why. I guess the construction on the kitchen ended, the restaurant got busy, they started taking on more weekend work, Sunday brunches, wedding receptions, that type of thing. I'd bring it up sometimes, the idea of going down there, and they'd just smile at me weakly and say, well yes, maybe next week, or the week after, but of course the next week they'd be busy again.

I think the last time I actually went down there with one of them was last November when Rebecca invited me to come along with her to do some Christmas shopping in midtown. It was one of those cold, overcast days, windy, as it always seems to be in the city that time of year, but it ended up being a very nice visit. We went to Saks and Barneys, stopped in at one of our favorite diners for pastrami sand-wiches, had a couple of cocktails at the Chelsea Hotel, and were on the train back to Rhinebeck before David had even noticed we were gone. On the ride home, I remember thinking to myself how lucky I was to have someone like Rebecca in my life, someone who I could spend an afternoon with like this, but when I found myself telling her this—I was still feeling a little caught up in the nostalgia of the day, a little drunk—she just looked out the window absently and smiled. Later, as we were pulling in closer to Poughkeepsie, she asked me out of the blue if I remembered the night in college when we'd kissed. This was before she'd gotten together with David, maybe about a month or so before, and it had been a strange, meaningless thing, a drunken kiss at a party, but still, I wondered why she was bringing it up now, after all these years, when she never had before. She said that she'd really liked me back then and then asked me if I knew this. I told her I didn't, and then laughed, making a joke about missing my big chance.

"You really did." She smiled.

"Well," I said after a while, turning my head toward the window and looking out, "we all make mistakes, right?"

"Yes," she said, resting her head on my shoulder and sighing, "we certainly do."

It was a few days after that trip to New York that David pulled me aside one night at the restaurant and told me that he needed me to give them a little distance for a while, a little space. I wasn't really sure what he meant by this, or what had prompted it, but I could tell that he was serious. We were standing in the back of the restaurant just before the evening service, and I could see that he was frazzled. He walked over to one of the windows and looked out, then came back and put his arm around me. None of this had anything to do with me, he assured me. It was all about them. They just needed some time alone to work some stuff out.

I told him that I understood, of course, and then went home that night and called up my mother and told her I'd be coming home for the holidays. I ended up spending about a month down in Pennsylvania, staying first with my mother, then with my sister, then with an old friend from high school who had recently divorced. When I finally got back to Rhinebeck, a few weeks later, I gave them another couple days before I called, and when I did, it was like nothing had ever changed. We all went out to dinner together that night and they told me how much they'd missed me and how they never should have told me to give them distance because it wasn't really about me anyway, it was about them, and how their lives were so much better now that I was back.

Later that night, David and I walked back to Fontaine, which was closed for the Christmas holiday, and sat down at one of the tables in the back with a bottle of wine that he'd been saving for a special occasion. I could tell it was one of those bottles—the type that could have easily covered my rent—but I didn't say anything about this. I enjoyed it, and we talked for a few hours about all sorts of things, our college days, his marriage, his regrets about never having kids, opening a new bottle each time the conversation hit a lull, and then toward the end of the night, he started to talk about the Austin thing again, kind of obliquely at first, then more specifically, about how he'd actually flown down there while I was away and met with a few of the people he'd been talking to and how the wheels were now beginning to turn, metaphorically, at least.

As he spoke, though, I could tell that something was off—he seemed anxious, uncertain—and when he finally finished, I asked him if he was really sure that this was what he wanted, if Austin was what he wanted.

"I'm sure it's what Rebecca wants," he said, and shrugged.

I looked at him. "Have things really been that bad between you two?"

He paused and sipped his wine. "Do you think I can crash at your place tonight?"

"Is that your way of saying yes?"

"That's my way of saying I don't want to talk about it."

Over the years, David has stayed over at my apartment from time to time—sometimes if he's had a little too much wine to drink, sometimes if he has to go in early to work, but mostly when he's had a fight with Rebecca. In a strange way, I kind of look forward to these nights, not that I like it when they fight, just that it's one of the few occasions when David and I actually get a chance to talk. That night, though, I could tell that he was too far gone to do any more talking, so I rolled out the futon for him and covered him in blankets and then I went into my bedroom, crawled into bed, and called up Rebecca.

It was almost 3:00 a.m. by then, but when she finally answered, she didn't seem at all surprised to hear from me.

"Sorry to call so late," I said. "I just wanted to let you know your husband's here."

"And he's alive?"

"Barely, but yes. He's currently passed out on my couch."

"Thanks for calling."

"You okay?"

"I can't sleep," she said. "I keep having this feeling something really bad is about to happen. Do you ever feel like that?"

"All the time."

"So what do you do about it?"

"I try to ignore it."

"I wish I could," she said, and then was silent for a while. I thought of asking her about what was going on with David, about why they needed that time alone, but instead I brought up Austin and what David told me, how it seemed like things were getting serious now.

"Yeah," she said, sighing, "he seems to think so. I don't know. He's somehow convinced himself that this is what I want and that it will somehow solve everything."

"Everything?"

"In our marriage."

"And what do you think?"

"I don't know," she said. "Some days I think it will, some days I'm not so sure." She sighed. "But I guess this is his way of making a grand gesture, right?"

I turned off my bedside lamp and lay there for a while in the dark, listening to Rebecca breathing. Outside my window I could see snow falling still, big soft flakes swirling in the wind.

"I wish we were still in college," she said. "I'd ask you on a date."

"We already went on a date in college, remember?"

"That wasn't a date," she said. "That was a hookup. I mean a proper date. Like at a nice restaurant. Maybe a movie after."

"I'm sure I'd only disappoint you," I said.

"That's impossible," she said, and I could hear her voice fading a little, drifting off into sleep. "I really don't think that's possible, Rich."

I lay there for a while longer, listening to her breathing, unsure of whether she'd fallen asleep or not, and then at one point, after I'd thought she'd drifted off, she started to speak again, just softly.

"You know I'm going to leave him, don't you?"

"What are you talking about?"

"Maybe not this year, maybe not next, but someday."

"You've said that before."

"Yes," she said, "but this time I mean it."

"You guys are in a rough patch. You've had rough patches before."

"Yeah," she said, "but not like this." She paused then, and I could hear her breathing again, slowly. "You know what scares me the most though? It's that I don't even know what it is anymore. I mean, it's not like he cheated on me or something. That would be easy. That would be something I could point to."

"What do you think is going to happen when you get to Austin?"

"I think we'll probably split up." She paused. "But we still have to try it, right?"

"Why?"

"Just to see," she said. "Maybe I'm wrong."

"I've never heard you talk like this before. Are you drunk or something?"

"I might be."

"David's your best friend."

"I know," she said, and sighed. "He's my whole life."

. . .

The next morning David was gone when I woke up, but later that night, after the evening service had ended, he stopped by again, this time sober and full of contrition. He said that there was a lot more to the Austin story than what he'd originally told me. Then he asked me if he could come in.

It was close to midnight by then, and outside the snow was starting to come down heavily, so heavily that I worried he might have to stay over again, but when I shepherded him inside, he said that he could only stay for a few minutes, maybe half an hour tops. He looked around the apartment nervously. Then he peeled off his coat and laid it down on the couch.

Later, as we sat over drinks in my kitchen, he began to explain it to me, just briefly, how he'd decided to put in an offer on a space in Austin—a restaurant space in the downtown area—and how that offer had originally been rejected, but then later accepted. He then went on to explain how he had also been approached by a number of investors around the same time, investors from Manhattan, and how two of these investors had actually made an offer on Fontaine. It had all happened very quickly, he said, the whole thing, quicker than he'd expected, but it did seem to be happening now. I asked him what this meant and he said that it meant that things were moving along at a slightly faster clip than he'd originally imagined and that they were looking at summer now, summer or fall.

"Summer?"

"Yes.

"To move?"

"Yes." He nodded.

"What happened to two years from now?"

He looked away.

I asked him how long he'd known this and that's when he grew evasive. He turned toward the window and looked out at the falling snow.

"We were worried about telling you," he said.

"Why?"

He stared at me.

"I'm not a child," I said.

"For what it's worth Rebecca wanted to tell you months ago, so if you're going to get mad at anyone—"

"If I'm going to get *mad* at anyone?"

"Yes," he said, "if you're going to get mad at anyone—"

But I wasn't listening anymore. I can't even remember what I said to him. All I remember was walking into my bedroom and closing the door, and then later, when I came out, finding David gone and a note on the counter, a note I didn't read.

All night long my cell phone kept ringing, but I didn't pick it up. I knew it was Rebecca, and I knew what she wanted. I knew what she was going to say, but I didn't want to hear it. To be honest, I wasn't even really sure what I was feeling at that moment. Angry that I'd been lied to, annoyed that they'd felt the need to protect me from this information, sad that it actually seemed to be happening now, this thing that I'd somehow convinced myself would never happen. It was all a lot to process.

I poured myself another glass of wine and then lay down on the sofa and closed my eyes. The phone kept ringing, every five minutes or so, and I kept ignoring it, and then finally, around one, I lost my resolve and picked up. Rebecca's voice sounded hollow and distant on the other end, like she'd just woken up from a nap.

"I'm sorry," she said. "I told him we should tell you at Christmas."

"You've known since Christmas?"

She was quiet on the other end.

"What about all of that stuff you said last night?"

"What stuff?"

"About leaving him?"

She was quiet again for a long time. "I must have been drunk," she said. "Did I really say that?"

"Becky."

"Look Richard," she said. "Just promise me you don't hate me."

"I don't hate you."

"And promise me you'll come with us."

"I can't come with you."

"Why not?"

"You know why not. I can't."

"We've never been alone without you," she said.

"I know," I said, "maybe that's the problem." I paused then. "Besides, what happens if I move down there and then the two of you break up?"

"David says that if you move down there, the chances of that happening are less."

"Well, I'm not going to move down there just to save your marriage," I said, and as soon as I said these words I realized how strange they sounded, how strange my life had become.

"Look," I said. "You and I both know that this was never part of the plan anyway."

"What?"

"Me coming along with you. I mean, tell me honestly that that was ever part of the plan."

She was quiet then for a long time and, in her silence, the question was answered.

· · ·

I have an album under my bed filled with old pictures of the three of us from college and from our first few years in New York. I used to look at it all the time, back when it used to make me feel better to look at such things, to stare at those old photos of our younger selves. But now it no longer does. If anything, it frightens me now to know it's there. The last time I looked at it, maybe two or three years ago, I was shocked at how different we looked and how happy we seemed. I remember flipping through it with a growing sadness until at one point I realized I was crying and had to put it away. I haven't looked at it since.

Still, there's one photo in that album that's always stayed with me. It's of the three of us, sitting in my old apartment on MacDougal, drinking wine. It must have been winter because we're all wearing our heavy winter coats, and David's wearing a hat, and Rebecca's wearing ear muffs, and I'm wearing mittens, and we're all turning our heads toward the camera and blowing, just to show how cold it is, our breath frozen in the air like mist, and what's funny about that photo is that I remember how cold it used to get back in that old apartment on MacDougal—the heating system was always breaking—but I have no memory of that actual day, and I have no memory of the person who took the picture. It makes me wonder how many other little things like that have simply disappeared from my mind, how many other little memories like that have simply vanished.

It's been two weeks now since all of this happened—since I first found out about the Austin move—and I sometimes wonder if the memory of this time will vanish, too, if the memory of these days, our last in Rhinebeck, will one day disappear.

Earlier today, I stopped by the new tapas place across the street from Fontaine. I sat at the window and watched across the street as the wait staff at Fontaine got ready for the evening service. I could see Colette and Rebecca talking at the bar, and at one point I noticed Rebecca looking out the window at me. It was snowing pretty hard outside, so I couldn't tell if she saw me staring back, but after a while she turned away and didn't look back again. Now, sitting at home, I wonder if I should have gone over and spoken to her, let her apologize. I wonder if I owed her that.

Before I go to sleep, I check my phone and see that there are two new voice messages—one from Rebecca and one from David. I could check these messages now or I could wait until the morning. Or I could simply erase them and never look back. It's strange to be forty-three years old and have no clue what the future might hold, to realize that you might have stepped onto the wrong train at some point in your life and somehow ended up in a place you hadn't expected or wanted or even known about when you were young. It's akin to waking up from a dream, I think, only to discover that you yourself were not the dreamer. But even so, I can still remember certain things, like I remember back in New York, when we were all so young and just starting out, how I'd stop by their apartment in the late evenings, usually after a long night of drinking with other friends, and how there would always be this moment when I'd come around the corner on Eighty-Sixth Street and see the edge of their apartment building and feel this kind of nervous excitement, not knowing if they were still awake, but hoping they were, and then the sense of comfort I'd feel when I'd finally see the light on in their second floor unit and realize they were home. It seemed like such a simple thing back then, but I still remember it now, that sense of anticipation as I walked up to the foot of their building and rang the buzzer, and the sight, a few seconds later, of one of their faces in the window, looking down at me and smiling, then waving me up, and then finally the sound of one of their voices, usually Rebecca's, on the intercom, telling me that they'd just opened up a bottle of wine and that I should come right in, that it must be freezing out there.

Chili

If you live in San Antonio long enough, you begin to develop a tolerance for heat; and I'm not just talking about the outdoor kind. I'm talking about jalapeños, and serranos, and habaneros. I'm talking about Chiles de Arbol and red savinas. For a few years in my early thirties I lived next door to an artist named Teresa who kept a whole garden of these chilis in her backyard. She had a lot of different varieties, some very obscure, some strange hybrids of various types of peppers indigenous to New Mexico and Texas. When she had people over she'd often pick a small bowl of these peppers and bring them back to the house, spread them out in a neat row on the kitchen table. She'd point at different peppers and say, "Oh, that one's nice." Or, "You want to stay away from that one. It'll bite you." Teresa was probably close to eighty at the time. She'd grown up in the Rio Grande Valley but had lived in San Antonio for most of her life, surviving as an artist by cobbling together various fellowships and grants, the occasional small commission or sale, a teaching opportunity here or there. In the evenings, I'd often see her working out in the small studio behind her house, a tiny white stucco building with a red-tiled roof that her second husband had apparently designed for her, back when they were still living together, back when they were still married.

When she'd eventually emerge from this studio in the late evenings, she'd often wave to me if I was still out on my back porch and invite me over. Sometimes she'd invite other people from the neighborhood over as well, and we'd all bring whatever beer we could find in our fridges and convene around her kitchen table. As for Teresa, she'd supply the music—usually some type of folk music from the 1960s (I remember her playing a lot of Joni Mitchell and Joan Baez)—and, of course, the chili peppers, usually several plates of them, if it was a big group. I can still remember one evening in early August—this must have been during that last summer I lived there—Teresa pointing out this very small, inconspicuous-looking red pepper and warning everyone to stay away from it. Usually, she joked about her peppers, but not this time. She was deadly serious. She said it probably wasn't even responsible for her to bring this pepper into the house where somebody might eat it by accident, but still, she said, she wanted everyone to see it. Wasn't it beautiful? she wondered. Wasn't it just perfect? And it was. Small and shiny and red, like a miniature bell pepper. She said it was the hottest pepper she'd ever grown, a unique hybrid of a Trinidad Moruga Scorpion and something else. She didn't have a name for it yet, she said. She was simply calling it "el diablo."

Using tongs, she placed it in the middle of the table where we could all see it better and we all just stared. "Don't even touch it," she said. "And definitely don't let it get close to your eyes."

Having lived next to Teresa for a while, I'd developed a bit of a tolerance for heat. I didn't think twice about eating a habanero, for example, or even a ghost pepper, which I'd tried twice. But this "el diablo" was something different I could tell. This wasn't a pepper you messed with.

As the night went on and we drank more beers, we gradually worked our way through the other peppers at the table, every one but "el diablo." It remained there in the middle of the room, solitary and untouched, even as people began to leave and Teresa cleared the table. She kept it there, as if not wanting to say goodbye to it yet.

In a year from then Teresa would be diagnosed with breast cancer, and within two years she'd be gone, but for some reason, whenever I think of her, I still think about that night, the sight of her sitting at her kitchen table by herself, drinking a cold beer and smoking a cigarette (she'd never quit), staring at her beautiful red pepper, as if it were the child she'd never had, or a painting she'd always wanted to make, this tiny, beautiful thing, so full of heat it might kill you.

Breathe

In the first few months of our son's life, when we were both completely exhausted, but also in a state of bliss, a state of constant delight and awe, a sort of floating euphoria that passed between us in waves, that made us remark with some frequency about how fucking amazing this all was, wasn't it, in those months I used to occasionally feel it— a shortness of breath, a panic, a fleeting nervousness that would enter my body like a current and then exit just as suddenly. I'd once asked my wife if she ever felt the same thing, a sort of mini panic attack from time to time, but she said she didn't. *Not ever?* No. Then later, when our son was two, it happened with greater frequency, once in the middle of a trip to the mall, my wife in the seat beside me. I'd pulled over on the side of the road and put my face in my hands.

"What's the matter with you?" she'd said. "Are you okay?"

I'd closed my eyes for a long time, pressed my hands to my forehead, and then, once my breathing had slowed, I'd looked at her and shook my head. "I don't know," I said. "I really have no idea."

The last time I'd felt anything like this—like what I used to feel before these attacks—was last summer when we were coming back from a birthday party at the house of one of our son's friends. The birthday party was a pool party, and there were probably about a dozen six-year-olds there, all of them accompanied by a parent or guardian, most of them wearing personal flotation devices of some sort. It was a pretty typical party. The parents on one side of the pool, the kids on the other, but then at one point—I don't know, maybe an hour or so into the party—there was a scuffle, some roughhousing and splashing at the far end of the pool, and our son, Ian, who was only five, who had never taken a swimming lesson in his life, slipped off the raft he was lying on and went under. Just for a few seconds, maybe less than three, but long enough for my wife, Kaitlyn, to scream out for me, a scream that was both panicked and accusatory—wasn't it she who said she would watch him? It didn't matter. In that moment I felt that sensation again, that sudden current shooting through me, and I stood there paralyzed, looking on from my spot at the food and drink table, a plate of sliders in my hand, standing motionless, as a sixteen-year-old girl, the sister of one of the other boys, quickly dipped down from her spot on the ladder and rescued my son.

Ian came up coughing water, a little frightened, but otherwise fine, and Kaitlyn quickly wrapped him in a towel and shepherded him away toward the house, while I remained at the food table, still in mid-bite, watching on like every other parent, like the boy who had almost just drowned wasn't my son.

.   .   .

Later, on the ride home, I said little to Kaitlyn, and she said little to me. Ian sat in the backseat watching a cartoon on Kaitlyn's phone. The day was beautiful, and I had the windows down and the radio going as we cruised along the dam and then later passed into the quiet, tree-lined streets of our neighborhood. I remember Kaitlyn leaning her head against the passenger side window at one point, closing her eyes, as she listened to the music, and Ian sitting behind her, perfectly still, staring at the cartoon on her phone. We passed along the river basin and then the athletic fields attached to the high school and then at some point shortly after that, as we were stopped at a stoplight, Ian started coughing—at first very lightly, then more violently. I knew about secondary drowning—how a child who has inhaled water can die even hours after going underwater—and for some reason that was the first thought that entered my mind. I said something about this to Kaitlyn, and she looked very seriously at Ian. He had stopped coughing by then.

"Are you okay, honey?"

He nodded.

"Are you sure?"

"Yeah."

"Did you cough up water?"

"No."

"It was just regular coughing?"

"Yeah."

Kaitlyn looked back at me. "I think he's okay," she said.

The light must have changed by then because I could hear the sound of cars honking behind me, but at that moment I felt powerless to do anything. My mind was racing. I was trying to figure out the fastest way to get to the nearest hospital with an emergency room, I was picturing Ian slipping under the water again, only this time there was nobody there.

"Gavin," Kaitlyn said. "We have to go."

The honking grew louder, but when I looked up at the light it was red again. There was the sound of voices behind me, then I turned and Kaitlyn was now at the driver's window rapping on the glass. I rolled down the window.

"Get out," she said.

"What?"

"Get out!" she said, opening the driver's door, and now I could hear the sound of people shouting again, behind us. "Jesus Christ, Gavin. Get out!"

At home, later that night, I tried to explain to Kaitlyn that it was just one of those things, a panic attack like I used to get when Ian was younger, but Kaitlyn didn't want to hear it. She said that she just needed a little time to decompress. She'd opened a bottle of wine and taken a glass out to the back deck with a cigarette, an occasional indulgence that she allowed herself on especially stressful days. Ian was in the family room watching TV. Usually we only allowed him one show per day, but that day, given what had happened, we had told him he could watch as many shows as he liked. Kaitlyn had made him some macaroni and cheese and chicken fingers, and he was now eating them out of a little plastic plate perched on the arm of the family room couch.

I walked into the room and sat down beside him.

"What are you watching?" I said.

His eyes remained on the set, as he mumbled something, the name of a show I'd never heard of. There were so many new shows these days, cartoon characters I'd never encountered before. Back when he was younger—maybe about two or three—he was obsessed with *Sesame Street*, and I had felt on familiar ground. I had known what he was watching, understood it. Lately, though, his interest in cartoons seemed to change almost daily. What he liked one day, he didn't like the next.

Today he was watching a Japanese cartoon with subtitles, an animated girl on a motorcycle cruising through the streets of some dark, futuristic city at night. There were villains shooting at her from car windows, violent explosions.

"What age is this for?" I asked.

He shrugged.

"Did Mom say you could watch this?"

He shifted on the couch and craned his head, so I wasn't blocking his view. Lately, he was in a non-speaking phase with me, not just when he was watching TV, but also on the way to school, in the morning at breakfast, in the evenings at dinner. Kaitlyn had told me it was normal, something all kids went through at different times. *He's in a mommy phase,* she'd said to me when I first brought it up, this sudden coldness. *It's totally normal.*

At night, I'd often eavesdrop on them reading books together, doing puzzles, always laughing. They'd had a special bond ever since Ian was born, and I'd always felt a bit on the outside of it, but during those first few years of Ian's life I had felt a closeness with him, too. I'd actually been out of work for the first two years of his life, and so we'd spent a lot of time together, going on play dates, hanging out at the park, taking day trips to various towns outside of San Antonio. I felt like we had built this thing together that would last throughout his teenage years and beyond, a special bond that most working fathers didn't get to share with their sons, but lately—at least in the past year or so, ever since I'd started working again, now at a much larger accounting firm downtown—Ian had started pulling away from me, asking for his mother, instead of me, requesting special nights with just her. *He wants to go out to dinner with just me,* Kaitlyn would say apologetically, when I'd call her from work, asking about dinner plans. *Is that okay?* And I'd tell her it was, sure.

"This will eventually pass," she'd tell me later in a reassuring voice, as we lay in bed. "If we had a daughter, it would probably be just the opposite."

And I'd nod and say, *sure, of course,* though sometimes I wasn't so sure.

Now, as Ian sat on the edge of the couch, his mouth covered with ketchup, staring ahead blankly at the television set, I felt a sudden and inexplicable need to hold him, but when I reached out for his shoulder, he moved away, recoiled, and then reached for another chicken finger. I looked out the sliding glass doors of our family room and saw Kaitlyn watching me. She gave me a sympathetic shrug, a plaintive smile. Then she raised the glass of wine to her lips and looked away.

I'm not sure how much time passed after that. It was maybe an hour or so, maybe less. I was out in the kitchen, making some coffee, and Kaitlyn was on the other side of the house, taking a shower. Ian was still in the family room, watching TV. There was the sound of laughter on the TV, and then I heard Ian coughing again.

It was similar to the way he'd coughed in the car, but a little louder, a little more violent, and I immediately ran into the family room to find him bending over on the couch clutching his stomach.

"Hey buddy," I said, rushing up to him, and again I had an image of the pool, the girl pulling him up. *Like a seal,* I'd thought at that moment his head had gone under and then come up. He'd looked like a seal. "Hey buddy," I said, now grabbing his shoulders. "You okay?"

He coughed twice more, then nodded.

I called for Kaitlyn, but she was in the shower.

"You sure?"

"I'm fine, Dad," he said, and now in a voice that bordered on annoyance, "You need to stop freaking out."

His words, and the expression on his face, were so adult-like, so teenager-like, it almost frightened me.

He sat back down on the couch, and I could see he still had ketchup on his face. I picked up a napkin and went to wipe it off—it was such an instinct by then—and he jerked away.

"I'm not a baby," he said, pushing at my hand.

"You have ketchup on your face."

"Leave me alone."

"Let me get it," I said, and as I reached out again he struck me hard on the forearm.

I could hear the shower go off now, and I called for Kaitlyn again. I stared at his eyes. I was angry, but also worried. I wanted to see that everything was all right in there.

"Say you're sorry," I said after a moment.

"I'm not sorry."

Just then Kaitlyn came into the room, her body wrapped in a towel, her wet hair combed back in rows.

"What's going on?" she said.

"He was coughing again," I said, turning to her. "And he hit me."

"You hit your father?" Kaitlyn said sternly now, and Ian looked down, melted back into the couch. Kaitlyn walked over to the TV and turned it off.

"I think it's time for you to go to bed," she said to Ian, but he wasn't looking at her. He was looking at me, looking at me with such an intense hatred I can still picture it even now, months later. It was as if he believed that by staring at me in this way he could make me disappear.

"Would you like me to help you get ready for bed?" I offered at one point, feeling suddenly guilty, but he was already standing up by then and walking toward the hall.

"No," he said, his voice trailing down the dark corridor. "I would not."

Looking back now, it's hard to say exactly when things with Ian began to change. I know that when he was about four years old we went on a trip back East to visit Kaitlyn's parents, and when we returned from this trip he was different. Suddenly he wanted Kaitlyn to read to him at night, wanted Kaitlyn to get him dressed. It didn't occur to me that anything profound had happened, though, until about a month or so later when he suddenly stopped talking to me altogether, when he suddenly stopped answering my questions at breakfast, stopped asking me to help him with his shoelaces, his artwork. He would walk around the house as if in constant avoidance of me, ducking into his bedroom whenever he saw me, looking down whenever he passed me in the hall. When I would suggest going out into the backyard to kick the soccer ball around, he'd look at me askance or feign fatigue, then retreat into some other part of the house or flop down on the couch, covering his eyes, waiting for me to leave. Later, when I'd try to talk to him about it, about his avoidance, he'd act as if he had no idea what I was talking about. He'd sit there on the couch, blank-faced, staring at me, trying to wait it out, knowing that eventually, if he waited long enough, I'd get tired and give up.

I asked Kaitlyn what she thought was going on and she said she wasn't sure. She agreed it was strange but thought it would pass. I asked his teachers at school if they noticed anything different in his behavior, but they said they didn't. They said he was doing great; he was a happy kid. They said he volunteered regularly for class activities, that he had lots of friends. They said he was one of the smartest and most well behaved students in the class.

I was thinking about this later that night, as I lay in bed, surfing the internet, reading whatever I could find about secondary drowning. Ian had had two more brief coughing episodes by then, short in duration but loud in intensity, and Kaitlyn had agreed that we should probably try to keep an eye on him tonight.

He was in his room now, trying to sleep. I looked over at Kaitlyn, who was standing in the doorway of our closet. I told her what I'd found, how I'd ruled out whooping cough (he'd been immunized) and asthma, as he'd only just started coughing today. It also seemed unlikely that it was the flu or some type of virus, as it wasn't a phlegmy cough, and he hadn't shown any other signs of illness.

Kaitlyn walked over to the bed and sat down on the edge. "If you're worried it's secondary drowning, then take him to the emergency room."

I stared at her. "I can tell you don't believe me, though."

"It's not about believing you," she said. "If that's what you think it is, then that's what you should do." She stared at me as if this were a threat. The last time we'd taken Ian to the emergency room, it had been a false alarm—I'd overreacted to a sudden spike in his temperature—and it had cost us about a thousand dollars simply because of the way our new insurance policy was structured. I knew this was what she was alluding to, tacitly, when she smiled.

"I know it's unlikely," I said.

"Highly unlikely," she said.

"Yes, highly unlikely, but it does happen." I looked at her. "I'm just saying the timing of it all. I mean, he wasn't coughing at all this morning, right?"

She stood up and walked over to the closet again. "And we're monitoring that, aren't we?"

"We are. Yes."

She disappeared into the closet, and I could hear her pulling down some boxes from one of the top shelves.

"By the way," I said. "Why wasn't he wearing his floaties?"

"When?"

"When he went under?"

She continued to pull down the boxes but said nothing. "Do you really want to get into this?" she said finally.

"What?"

"Whose fault it was."

I said nothing.

A moment later, she came out of the closet and without looking at me walked across the room, paused momentarily at the door, then closed it firmly behind her.

For the next two hours, there was no sound at all from Ian's room. It was now after midnight, Kaitlyn had long since gone to sleep on the couch (a not so subtle message to me that she was still upset), and I was still lying in bed reading over the articles I'd pulled up from the internet—from various medical sites and parenting sites and blogs.

Some of the information I'd found was contradictory, some of it a little frightening. I'd gone to check on Ian about four or five times in the past hour or so, and he seemed fine, sleeping soundly. I was still thinking about the way he'd struck me earlier, the way he'd stared at me. I could understand him being more attached to Kaitlyn—that was natural, after all—but what I couldn't understand was his intense disdain for me. The therapist I'd gone to see a couple of months earlier had thought it might be a projection thing, that he was projecting something onto me or that I was projecting something onto him. *Fathers and sons*, the therapist had said vaguely, as if there were a world of meaning in that statement. And then he'd looked down at his watch and said our time was up.

That afternoon I'd picked up Ian early from school and taken him to a restaurant in our neighborhood, a taco place that he loved. I told him he could order whatever he wanted, but he said he wasn't hungry. Later, on the way home, I suggested stopping by a bookstore near the university that we used to go to when he was younger, a kind of ritual we had, but he said that he already had enough books.

"How about the park?" I said, but he just closed his eyes.

"You need to stop doing this, Dad."

"Doing what?" I said.

And then, in his mysteriously adult way, he waved his hands above his head and said, "This. You need to stop doing *this*."

It was probably about three or four in the morning when I heard the coughing again—definitely his loudest fit yet, though it didn't wake Kaitlyn, who was still fast asleep on the couch.

When I got to the doorway of Ian's room, he was already sitting up in bed, clutching his stomach.

"Dad," he said, and I could see he was scared.

"I think we should go to the hospital," I said.

He nodded.

But instead of picking him up and getting him dressed, I walked over to the bed and sat down beside him. I put my arm around him and he let me. I thought about Kaitlyn and what she would say if this latest trip was another false alarm, another thousand-dollar false alarm, and I began to doubt myself again. I thought about what I'd said to the therapist—how I had a tendency to make things up, to imagine sudden illnesses that weren't really there, to create in my mind unrealistic scenarios whereby Ian was harmed or infected in some way, how it was my nature, since he'd been born, to imagine the worst.

"How are you feeling now?" I said to Ian.

He looked down at his hands.

"Do you want to lie down for a second?"

"I thought we were going to the hospital."

"We might," I said. "But let's just rest for a second first."

He looked at me skeptically, then closed his eyes and lay back gradually on the bed.

I turned off the light on his bedside table, and as soon as he heard the click, he opened his eyes and told me to turn it back on.

"Why did you do that?" he said.

"Just relax."

I could see that his forehead was damp and reached down and brushed away his bangs. Again, he let me.

"Don't turn out the lights," he said.

"Okay."

"Why is this happening?" he said. "Why do I keep coughing?"

"I don't know," I said. Then I thought about one of the articles I'd read online. "Does it hurt," I said. "When you cough?"

"A little."

"Just try to relax," I said. "Close your eyes."

And this time he did, he kept them closed, and I sat there for a while, maybe twenty minutes or so, watching him, wondering what to do. I knew that I couldn't keep freaking out like this every time something happened. I knew that we couldn't afford to keep indulging my anxieties. But at the same time I was having trouble reconciling the facts, the coincidence of it all, the timing. I thought about the urgent care center less than a mile from here, but we'd had bad experiences with them and I didn't trust the doctors there completely. They'd be cheaper, of course, but also less reliable. I also thought about the fact that in less than five hours from now his pediatrician's office would be opening and I could just call them up, maybe even bring him over, but five hours from now seemed like a long time. I stared at his face, trying to determine if it was paler, bluer. *Look out for blue lips and blue skin,* the article online had said. *Be concerned if you see foaming at the mouth.* I reached down and touched his arm, then tugged gently on his pajama sleeve, and this time he stirred, shifting in the bed. I did it again, and he looked up with a start, blinking until I came into view.

"How are you feeling now?" I said, touching his arm until he'd calmed.

"Okay," he said, and closed his eyes.

I touched his chest then and pressed it gently.

"Does that hurt?" I said.

"Stop it," he said and squirmed away.

"Lie still," I said and pressed on it again, using my other arm to keep him still.

"Stop it, Dad," he said, and turned away from me. He pulled his covers around his body and faced the wall. A moment later, lying in the fetal position, he started to cough again, a very loud, strained sort of cough, a wheezing cough, and when he finally stopped I could see he was shaken.

"Why is this happening?" he said again.

"I don't know," I said calmly, and then I sat down beside him and put my hand on his shoulder and he let me this time.

"I'll make you a deal," I said. "If you cough again, we go to the hospital. Okay? One more time and we go."

He nodded.

"Okay?"

"Yes."

I sat there then and watched him and for a while neither of us spoke, though Ian kept his eyes open, staring straight up at the ceiling, as if afraid that if he moved he might set off another coughing fit. I stared at his chest, monitored his breathing. *Look out for anything irregular*, the medical site had said. *Rapid and shallow breaths are a sign.* But Ian's breathing looked regular now. As normal as any other night. And I felt comforted for a brief moment by the quietness of the room, this dimly lit bedroom filled with posters of Spider-Man, and beautiful drawings Ian had made in preschool, and postcards from his uncles and aunts and grandparents thumbtacked to his bulletin board. He'd had a good life, this kid, much easier than my own childhood had been. He'd wanted for nothing. He had two parents who adored him. Lots of friends. He had a big backyard, every type of lesson you could imagine. And yet somehow there was still a sadness there, an unhappiness, a discontent. Where had it come from?

Perhaps it was only me he showed this unhappiness to, as if to let me know that it was my fault, that he was this way because of me. Or, perhaps it was much simpler than that. Perhaps he was simply disappointed with the hand that he'd drawn, the father he'd been given. Perhaps what he wanted most of all was simply another life.

Earlier that week, I'd mentioned something about this to Kaitlyn and she'd sighed and said that I needed to stop spending so much time thinking about my relationship with Ian and start spending more time trying to have one. She suggested pulling out a couple of my old photo albums from childhood and showing him all the places I had lived growing up. Fort Carson, Fort Benning, Fort Bragg. I think he'd be interested, she said, but when I showed him the photos of all the bases I'd grown up on, my sisters and me in our hand-me-down clothes, I could tell he didn't know what to make of it. *Why did you move around so much?* he'd asked at one point, eyeing a photo of our base home in Fort Sill, and when I explained to him that it wasn't really our choice, that that was how the military worked, he'd simply nodded and looked out his bedroom window and then asked if he could watch a show on his iPad. Later, when I went into the family room to check on him, he was lying with his head on Kaitlyn's lap, his eyes closed, a strange bemused smile on his face.

Now, though, lying in the dim light of his bedroom, his face looked anything but tranquil, bemused. His skin looked pallid, clammy, his forehead damp, his bangs plastered to his brow. I reached over to touch the skin above his eyes, and it was cool, even cold. I turned off the lights and watched his breathing.

Around me the room was dark but I could make out the shapes of his stuffed animals perched along the shelves and the smell of something musty, rank, a pair of gym shorts abandoned beneath his bed. I wondered if there might be water in Ian's lungs. I'd read several stories online about children taking naps, then simply passing away from secondary drowning. *I'd thought he was sleeping,* one quote had said. *I'd thought he was taking a nap.* I thought about the water being inside him, in a place it wasn't supposed to be, and I felt a tightening in my chest.

After a moment, I reached over and turned on his table lamp again. I touched his arm, tried to wake him, and it was only then, when he opened his eyes, and I saw that the skin around the edges of his eyelids was red and puffy, chafed, that I realized he'd been crying.

"Hey," I said, but he turned away.

"Hey, buddy, what is it?"

He was quiet for a long time and just lay there, staring at the ceiling. I thought of reaching out to him again, but didn't. Instead, I just sat there, watching him as he lay there quietly. He moved his hand along the side of his body, across his ribs, then let it rest on his chest. He closed his eyes, then opened them again.

Finally, he said, "Why weren't you there?"

"What do you mean?"

He continued looking up at the ceiling.

"Ian?"

"Why didn't you come help me?"

"When?"

"Afterward."

"After when?"

"In the pool. Why weren't you with me? You were supposed to be with me."

I looked at him, and I could see that he was not angry, but still scared, still shaken by what had happened.

"It was actually Mommy's—" I began, but then stopped myself. "You're right," I said. "I should have been there."

He continued looking up at the ceiling.

"Parents aren't always perfect," I said. "We mess up a lot. We're flawed individuals. Most of us at least." I knew that what I was saying probably wasn't registering, but I continued talking anyway. "I'm probably more flawed than most if we're being honest. But you're right. I should have been there. You're absolutely right about that."

He rubbed his eyes with the arm of his pajamas and looked away. "But what were you doing?" he said.

"What do you mean?"

"What were you *doing*?" he said. "What were you *do*-ing?"

I looked at him and then looked down at my hands but said nothing. I didn't have an answer for him. I wasn't sure if I ever would.

After a moment, Ian curled himself into the fetal position and pulled his legs to his chest and stared back at the wall.

He lay there like that for a long time, and it took me a while, almost several minutes, before I realized he wanted me to leave.

In the coming hours, Ian's cough would gradually subside, and by the time I took him into the pediatrician's office the next morning there was virtually no sign of it at all. We never really found out what it was. It was just one of those things, according to the pediatrician, a mild cold perhaps, a flu; maybe an allergy of some sort. There was really no way of knowing.

This is what would happen, but in that moment, as I sat there on his bed, I was still worried, still thinking the worst. And I remember waiting there in the darkness of his room, staring at his small face, his chest, thinking about what he'd said.

"What were you doing?" he'd said, and I knew what he meant. I knew he meant what had I been doing at the moment he went under or perhaps during the five or ten minutes before that, when he was lying on a raft by himself without floaties or any other type of flotation device. Me, troller of parenting blogs. Me, obsessive reader of parenting guides and parenting advice columns. What had I been doing at that moment, aside from making myself a slider? I had been at the food and drink table, but where had my mind been? What had

I been obsessing about at that particular moment that caused me to lose sight of my one primary responsibility as a parent: to keep my child alive. I tried to think back—tried to recall where I was mentally at that particular moment—but I honestly couldn't remember. All I could see was sunlight on the water, a quick glint, a bright flash, then nothing.

Silhouettes

At the beginning of last summer I was having dinner with my friend
Paul Bélanger—an old colleague from my days at Texas State—when
my wife, Amy, called to say that our dog had run off. She reported
this information with such equanimity in her voice, though, such
calm, that I knew immediately that our dog had not run off at all and
that she was calling me home for some other reason. In any event,
I told Paul that I had to go home to deal with this emergency, and
he was very kind about it, very understanding. He suggested that we
meet up again over the weekend if I was still up for tennis (we used to
have a weekly game) or maybe even an early brunch out in Westlake
Hills, which was where he was living now.

Paul is French Canadian, and his wife, Elaine, is from somewhere just north of here—Windemere, I think. Elaine comes from
money. I'm not sure how much, but it's considerable—enough that

they were able to recently purchase this large house out in Westlake Hills, a five-bedroom Arts and Crafts–style house overlooking a wet weather creek on one side and a canyon on the other. It's a beautiful house, no question, and very tastefully furnished. The first time they had us out there, Amy and me, I remember feeling amazed that I actually knew someone who could afford a house this size. Most of our other friends in Austin still rent.

Anyway, Amy had never really liked Paul and Elaine, though it had nothing to do with their money. What bothered her was the fact that she felt that Paul had somehow backstabbed me when I'd gone up for tenure at Texas State a few years back. This was when we were both still colleagues in the Department of Psychology and fairly close friends. The department's vote had apparently been split, with seven voting for me, eight against. We'd been able to deduce who would have probably voted for me and who would have likely voted against, but there were still a couple of votes we couldn't account for, swing votes, I guess, and Amy felt sure that one of those votes had been from Paul.

Of course, Paul had claimed that he'd argued adamantly on my behalf, and I had believed him, at least at first. I had no reason not to; if anything, Paul's vote was the one vote I felt certain I could count on. But then he kept bringing it up, kept mentioning it, how hard he'd fought for me, and that's when I started to doubt it, or when Amy had started to doubt it, really. One night, shortly after my second and last appeal had been rejected, Paul and Elaine were over for dinner, and Paul kept talking about it, almost like he was trying to get something off his chest. We were all a little drunk, and maybe that's why it seemed so transparent—I don't know—I just remember Amy coming up behind me in the kitchen as I was making us dessert and coffee, and saying, "Jesus, he's totally fucking lying."

"I know," I said before I'd even considered what I was saying.

"I can't believe it," she said.

I walked over to the cabinet above the stove where we kept our wine. "I think I need more wine."

Amy started pacing around the kitchen. "What do we do now? Kick them out? Confront him?"

"No," I said. "We have dessert, and then we say good night to them and then we never talk to them again."

"Okay," she said.

But of course that never really happened. The next week Paul called me up to invite me to a party, and I accepted; the week after that Amy and Elaine were going out together to some bar in Westlake Hills; and so on and so forth. Our lives continued in much the same way as they had before, only with this one slight difference: I now knew that Paul had betrayed me.

To be honest, it didn't really bother me when we were out together. I'd found a way to put it out of my mind, and Paul himself rarely mentioned it—my tenure case, that is. It seemed that after that one night at our apartment he'd decided to stop bringing it up. Maybe he'd realized how transparent he'd looked. Or maybe Elaine had said something to him. Who knows? I remember Amy once telling me that Elaine often alluded to what had happened to me in very cryptic terms, that she often hinted at Paul's guilt or the burden he was carrying, but said little else. It was almost as if she was trying to confess, Amy thought, trying to come clean.

Whatever. My life hadn't ended when my tenure case was denied, but it hadn't been easy either. It had taken me almost a full year to get another job in academia, and even then it hadn't been a job in my field, or in any academic field really. It had been an entry-level position in the marketing department of a small liberal arts college in the area. The salary was modest in comparison to what I'd been making as an assistant professor at Texas State, but after what I'd been through that past year, I was grateful to have it. Amy often reminded me of how much worse things could be—she'd been laid off from her own public radio job earlier that year, and for a while there we'd both been on unemployment—and though I often missed the classroom, and my spacious office, and my old research, I knew that she was right.

"He might have even done you a favor," she'd sometimes say, when I was feeling particularly depressed about it. "You never liked any of those people anyway."

And I'd nod and agree with her, but then sometime later, as I was standing by myself in the bathroom, looking in the mirror, or as I was walking our dog, Henry, around the block, I'd have an image of something—I'd see Paul and his beautiful house out in Westlake Hills, or I'd think of the graduate school loans I was still paying off, loans for a degree that I no longer needed—and I'd feel a throbbing in the back of my head, just behind my ears, a tightening in my gut. I'd realize that I was very capable of doing something terrible to Paul—that a part of me wanted to.

I wasn't feeling that way that night, though, when I came home to our apartment and found Amy lying half-asleep on our couch, her arm draped loosely around the head of our Border Collie, Henry, the other hand holding a glass of wine. She looked at me absently and smiled.

"I figured you'd want an out," she said. "It had been like, what, two hours?"

I nodded. "It wasn't actually that bad," I said. "Not like the last time."

The last time Paul and I had hung out, he'd talked almost incessantly about the department and the mistakes they were making, how they were losing majors left and right because of their unwillingness to embrace the new curriculum, and so forth, and though I knew he was only venting, that he wasn't actually thinking about me as he spoke, it was still hard to sit there and listen to him, to pretend that I still cared about these people who had essentially screwed me over.

"He wants us to come out there this weekend," I said. "Him and Elaine. He suggested brunch or maybe dinner."

"Let's do dinner," Amy said, "if we have to. Brunch is always so awkward."

"Or we could just cancel on them," I said.

"No." Amy sighed. "We should go. We've been blowing them off a lot lately."

I nodded and sat down on the chair across from her. I put up my feet on the ottoman. "Plus," I said. "This will give us a chance to add to our collection."

Amy shook her head and laughed. "*Your* collection."

This had been a running joke, a joke that had started about nine months ago when we came home from a party at their house, and I realized I'd accidentally put this antique bottle opener in my pocket while I'd been standing outside by the pool, opening beers for a group of people who were sitting around the fire pit. I'd made the mistake honestly of course, and yet the longer I stood there looking at it, the longer I held this antique bottle opener in my hands, the less inclined I felt to give it back. It had the look of a family heirloom, maybe something passed down from Elaine's parents, and I suddenly realized I wanted it, or at least that I wanted them not to have it anymore. The next time we went out there for an early dinner, I found myself taking a framed photograph of Paul and his brother, a photograph from their youth that I figured was probably pretty important to him, and the time after that I took a couple of old books from his personal collection, both first editions. Over the next few months, I took a number of other little things—a tasseled key chain, a pair of cuff links, one of Elaine's turquoise necklaces. If I came across something small on my way back from the bathroom, or as I was passing by their bedroom, I'd slip it into my pocket, and then later, at home, I'd pull it out and show it to Amy and she'd laugh and shake her head, and then I'd take it into the bedroom and put it in the little cardboard box I'd hidden under my bed.

If you had asked me then if I thought what I was doing was wrong I would have said no. In my mind, I think I believed that I would eventually give it all back, that I was simply keeping it for now, or other times I'd tell myself that it was a kind of retribution for what Paul had done to me. I had ways of justifying it to myself, and Amy herself never questioned it. We believed ourselves to be good people—and I still believe we are—but there was no way to really account for, or explain, the cardboard box that was sitting under my bed. Sometimes, late at night, as I lay there in the dark, restless from all of the anxieties in our lives, I'd think of that box right underneath me, those tiny pieces of Paul and Elaine's life that I'd taken from them, those inconsequential little mementos, those oddly personal trinkets and keepsakes, those little souvenirs and tokens that I'd somehow appropriated and given to myself out of envy, or perhaps out of anger, or maybe both. I'd think about that box and I'd wonder what it meant. I'd wonder if I was possibly losing my mind. Then, after a while, I'd close my eyes and I'd forget about it. I'd think of something else, and sometimes several days would pass—sometimes even a week—before I'd think of it again.

Now Amy was stretched out lengthwise on the couch, her eyes closed, her one free hand still resting on Henry's head. I walked over to her and sat down beside her. I put my hand on her shoulder, and after a while she looked up at me and sighed.

"Okay," I said, smiling, rubbing her back.

"What?"

"Okay," I said. "I'll tell them dinner."

The part of Westlake Hills where Paul and Elaine live is located just beyond the Wild Basin Preserve, a heavily wooded area with wonderful bike trails and great panoramic views of the Hill Country and downtown Austin. Whenever we go out there, it feels like we're entering another country. Sometimes we'll notice another car on their road or we'll see the faint light from one of their neighbors' houses through the trees, but for the most part when we're out there we feel completely removed from the world. As Paul once put it himself, that house and the acre or so of woods surrounding it, was the closest thing he could find to northern Quebec in Central Texas. "It's not the same at all, of course," he said to us one night, when we were over for dinner, "but sometimes late at night, when I've had enough wine, I can sit out on the back deck and pretend it is." Paul speaks with a slight French accent—an accent that would be hard for most people to place had they not known where he'd grown up—and when he said things like this it always seemed to come on stronger.

That night—the night he'd said this—we'd all been sitting out by the pool in their backyard, smoking cigarettes (an old habit for all of us) and looking out over the canyon in the distance. It was a clear night and very quiet, and the only thing you could really hear was the faint sound of music coming from a party at one of the other houses on their road. At one point, Amy had decided that it might be fun to try to find this party and crash it—this might give you some sense of how much wine we'd had with dinner—and Paul had agreed to join her. They'd gone off together through the woods, and Elaine and I had stayed out by the pool, smoking more cigarettes and drinking more wine, and then eventually stripping down to our underwear and getting in the water. I'd swum in my underwear at Paul and Elaine's many times before—it was practically a ritual at that point—and so I hadn't really thought a thing about it, not until about a half hour later when Paul and Amy returned—they'd apparently gotten lost or given up—and I'd seen this expression on Paul's face that I'd never seen before. It was an expression that told me I'd screwed up. Elaine and I had gotten out of the pool, and Paul and Elaine had gone off to talk. The evening had ended awkwardly, with Paul going into the bedroom by himself, and Elaine coming out in her bathrobe to say good night. "I'm sorry," she said, as we stood there in the front foyer of their house. "He's been going through a lot lately. I'm sure you can understand." And we told her we did, of course, and then we said good night to her and hugged her tightly and drove home, and the next time we saw them, almost two weeks later, there was no mention of anything that had happened that night.

I don't know why it was that I was thinking about this memory that night—that next Saturday—as we drove up the long wooded driveway to Paul and Elaine's house, but for some reason I was. For some reason it was stuck in my mind. Maybe it was because the quality of light that evening was so similar to the night I remembered—the sun descending just beyond the tall trees at the far end of their yard—or maybe it was something else, maybe it was the temperature in the air, the quietness of the woods. When we pulled up to their house, we had the windows down and I could smell the smoke from the fire pit on the side of their house, over by the canyon and the pool. The house itself was dark, though, almost all of the lights were turned off, and I had the funny feeling that we might have gotten the date wrong—that Paul might have said Sunday and not Saturday, or that he might have meant Saturday a week from now—but just as I was about to say something to Amy about this Paul emerged from the side of the house with an armful of kindling, smiling and shouting something I couldn't hear. He was dressed in his usual attire: running shorts and a T-shirt, an old pair of beaten-up Tevas. He looked youthful and fit for a man pushing fifty, his hair a regal silver, his skin perpetually tan. He had the limber physique of someone who had never eaten anything processed or fried, a man who had subsisted on couscous and fava beans and lean meats.

As we got out of the car, he came over to join us, his arms still holding the firewood, which made it difficult to hug him or shake hands. I leaned in to pat him on the back, awkwardly, and Amy did the same.

"How was traffic?" he said.

"Good," I said. "Manageable."

"Good," he said and smiled. Then he motioned for us to follow him across the lawn. "Come on," he said. "I have a surprise."

As we made our way across the lawn and down a slight incline toward the swimming pool and the stone deck, you could see the canyon come into view, the sun setting in the distance, and just beside that, to the left, a small patch of juniper trees and purple mountain laurels. Elaine was sitting in a large mesh chair on the other side of the patio area beside the pool, and across from her, at another table, were a man and woman whom I didn't recognize, a youngish couple who seemed about the same age as Amy and me. Elaine had put out some small tea light candles on the glass table and some white paper lanterns up in the branches of the loquat trees beside the pool and everything down there seemed ethereal and strange.

"Do you recognize them yet?" Paul was saying now, turning back to me and smiling, but I didn't. I'd never seen these people before in my life.

Paul motioned for us to keep walking, and then, as we moved

down a little closer, as we began to approach the small slope at the bottom of the hill, I started to realize who they were. The man was Garrett Long, an old colleague of ours from Texas State, a mutual colleague from the Department of Psychology who had come in during the same year as me, but left after only a year for a better job at UC Berkeley. Now Garrett was older, and slightly thinner, bearded. His wife, Lindsay, had been a good friend of Amy's—they'd taken a yoga class together—and during that one year they'd been here, we'd hung out a lot, the four of us. Now, as Lindsay was standing up to greet us, as she was pushing her chair away, I could see that she was pregnant, that she was probably in her second or third trimester.

"Holy shit," Amy said before I could even speak. "I can't believe it!" She ran over to Lindsay and the two of them embraced like sisters.

Garrett came over to greet me. "Steve," he said, pumping my hand. "Long time."

I felt a little disoriented, like I'd wandered into a dream someone else was having about me. I looked up at the house again, at the darkened windows, the empty carport. I wondered if this was some type of trick.

"I told Garrett, no talking shop tonight," Paul said, coming up behind me and putting his hand on my shoulder. He smiled. "I figured it was better to surprise you, right?"

"Sure."

"I hope it's okay."

"Of course," I said.

"I'm in town for a conference," Garrett explained.

"Oh yeah?" I said. "UT?"

"Yep."

"I'm afraid we've started without you," Elaine said, coming over to hug me now. She nodded at the empty wine bottles on the wall beside us.

"It's been a long afternoon," Garrett said, as if in apology.

"And poor Lindsay," Elaine said. "Having to sit here and listen to these two go on and on."

"On and on?" Paul said, frowning. "I take offense to that."

He motioned for us to sit down at the table and started to pour us each a glass of wine, all the while recounting some story that Garrett had told him earlier, a story that seemed to revolve around a series of random coincidences all connected to two people they both knew.

In a way, I was happy they'd all been drinking for a while. It took the edge off things and helped me relax a bit. I have to admit I felt a little blindsided. I knew that Paul would have never invited anyone over from the current department, not without my knowledge, but I guess that he figured Garrett was different. After all, Garrett and I had been friends; he'd had nothing to do with my tenure denial. He'd been long gone by then. But even so, it felt a little strange seeing him here. Clearly Paul would have told him what had happened to me. Clearly, he knew. We all sat down at the table where Elaine had been sitting and Paul began to uncork a few more bottles of wine, setting out a fresh set of glasses, then filling them up.

"So how far along are you?" Amy said to Lindsay now, taking one of the glasses Paul had filled.

"Eight months," Lindsay said.

"We're in the home stretch," Garrett added.

"The home stretch?" Lindsay laughed. "*We're* in the home stretch?"

"Sorry," he said. "My wife is in the home stretch." He smiled then and patted Lindsay's hand.

"This is actually our second," Lindsay said. "Our daughter, Alice, is back in Piedmont with her grandparents."

"You guys have been busy out in California," I said, smiling. Then, because it seemed only natural, I added, "So how's Berkeley?"

"Berkeley's good," Garrett said. "Berkeley's, you know—Berkeley."

I knew from Paul that Garrett had been doing well out there, that he'd been publishing a lot, that he'd recently received tenure, but I could sense that he was trying to downplay this now. He looked around the table vaguely, as if searching for a cue from Paul or Elaine, but nobody spoke. After a while, Elaine turned to me and smiled. "So, Steve," she said, "how's your dog?"

"Our dog?" I said.

"Did he ever come back? Paul told me he ran off."

"Oh right," I said, suddenly remembering. "He did. He came back that night." I looked over at Amy. "We're all together again, right?"

"That's right," Amy said and smiled.

The conversation continued like that for a while—awkwardly, haltingly—with no clear direction or purpose. It was obvious that Paul and Garrett were trying to avoid certain subjects, that they were trying to steer the conversation away from my time in the department, for example, or Paul's research or Garrett's accomplishments, all things that they probably figured I was sensitive about, but the problem was, without these common threads of interest, without these things that had initially bonded us all those years ago, there was not much to talk about.

After a while, Elaine excused herself to go up to the house to get the dinner, and Paul started talking about a movie he'd seen recently, a Dutch movie that he described as "very good, but very disturbing." He went on to try to summarize the plot of this movie, but I could tell by then that the day's intake of alcohol had finally caught up with him.

At one point he turned to Lindsay and said, "And then what happened?"

To which Lindsay started to laugh and took Paul's hand. "Paul," she said, "you're the only one here who's seen the movie. I have no idea what happened."

Paul looked around the table then and shook his head. "Oh fuck," he said. "I think I'm hammered."

This lightened the mood a bit, and everyone laughed, and then a moment later Elaine appeared on the lit path from the main house, holding a stack of aluminum containers in her arms. She made her way down the path tentatively, slowly, and after a while Garrett went up to help her, reaching out his arms to take several of the containers, and then guiding her down the hill with his voice. Before long, they were both back at the table again, peeling off the lids of the steaming hot containers and passing out napkins.

"This is from the Peruvian place down the road," Elaine said, as she pulled off one of the lids. "That place I was telling you about." She looked at Amy.

"Oh, right," Amy said and nodded.

"Vegetarian's on this side," she continued, motioning toward the far end of the table, "and the rest is right here. And don't let me forget, I have dessert back at the house for later."

She turned then to Paul and smiled, and then Paul turned to the rest of us and raised his glass. "Okay," he said. "Let's eat."

The dinner was amazing. Amy always makes fun of the fact that Paul and Elaine never cook, that they always order in when they entertain, but I've never minded. I've eaten at the houses of plenty of people who really shouldn't cook. At Paul and Elaine's you're always treated to a feast, and that night was no exception. In fact, the food was so good we barely spoke while we ate, little more than an occasional remark about how delicious the chicken was or how incredible the fried plátanos were. Papa rellena, arroz con pollo, these rich

Peruvian sausages. Most of us went back for seconds, and I think that Paul and Elaine went back for thirds. All the while we were drinking these incredible Syrahs from the Lompoc Valley outside of Santa Barbara that Paul claimed his older brother, Phil, had sent him.

Somehow between the food and the alcohol the mood began to change. Everyone began to relax a bit, open up, and at a certain point Paul began asking Garrett and Lindsay about their daughter, Alice, and then about parenting in general and what it had been like for them. He mentioned that he and Elaine had decided not to have children, but that they often second-guessed this decision, now that they were older. He looked around the table as he said this.

I'd never heard Paul say anything about this before—about children—and it surprised me. Maybe it was the alcohol or the lateness of the evening, but Lindsay and Garrett began to answer him honestly, saying that it had been very difficult for them but also rewarding, rewarding in ways they couldn't really explain. They said that one of the big mistakes that a lot of new parents make is expecting too much. They'd made that mistake themselves, Lindsay said, but now they'd learned to lower their expectations. She looked over at Garrett then and squeezed his hand.

"You know how everyone tells you that becoming a parent will change you and all?" she said. "Well, it does, of course, but just not in the way people make you think it will. It doesn't fill some big void or something. It doesn't solve anything. It just makes things different, you know? Sometimes better, sometimes worse. But mostly just different."

Lindsay turned back to Garrett then and prodded him into talking about some research study he'd read about, something about the relationship between happiness and parenting. He said that he didn't want to get into the technicalities, but that, yes, basically this group of graduate students and professors had done a fairly extensive study on the relationship between happiness and parenting and concluded that becoming a parent didn't actually make one happier. In fact, there was pretty compelling evidence that it made one less happy— in a general sense, at least.

"Which I could have told him." Lindsay smiled, patting her belly.

"You mean not ever?" Amy asked. "Or just when the kids are young?"

"No," he said. "Not even after the kids have left the nest. Not even when you're old and looking back on your life with nostalgia. Even then, those people who never had kids turned out to be happier."

"And healthier," Lindsay added.

"Right," Paul said. "And healthier."

"I don't know if I believe that," Elaine said. She looked perturbed. "I mean, how do you even measure happiness?"

"That's a fair point," Garrett said. Then he looked at Paul. "Sorry. I know we said no talking shop tonight."

"No," Paul said. "It's fine. It's interesting." Then he looked at Amy and me. "What about you two?"

"Do we want to have kids?" I said. "We're not opposed to the idea."

Amy elbowed me in the arm. "Yes," she added, "we do."

"Just not tomorrow," I said.

The truth was we hadn't talked about the issue of kids in several years, not since my tenure denial. For a long time things were so uncertain financially that it didn't seem responsible to even bring it up. Now, though, I could see in Amy's eyes that it wasn't a small issue for her. I reached across the table and squeezed her hand.

"Anyway," Lindsay said finally, picking up her water, "to answer the question you asked earlier, even if this research is true—and I'm not saying it is—but even if it is, it doesn't matter. Once you have a child, you can never imagine *not* having that child. So, in a sense, the issue of happiness is kind of irrelevant."

Garrett reached across the table for one of the wine bottles, but said nothing.

"I don't think the issue of happiness is ever irrelevant," Paul said vaguely, as if to himself, then he turned to Elaine, but she was already standing up and walking back toward the house. She yelled something back to us about getting dessert, but it was obvious that she was upset, that something about the conversation we'd been having had bothered her. A moment later, Paul stood up and said something about too much wine, how we'd all had too much wine, and then he started up the lit path after Elaine, running quickly to console her.

"Jeez," Lindsay said after Paul and Elaine had disappeared inside the house. "What was that?"

"Must have hit a nerve," Garrett observed.

"Don't worry about it," Amy said. "You couldn't have known."

"Known what?" I said.

"Elaine can't have children," she said and looked over at the loquat trees. "That's the reason they never have. It wasn't actually a decision."

"Really?" Lindsay said, squinting at Amy, and I stared at her too, surprised that she'd never mentioned this before.

Amy nodded.

I looked up at the house again, but everything was dark up there. I wondered where they were, what they were talking about.

"Anyone want more wine?" Garrett asked, looking around the table.

I held out my glass.

After he'd finished pouring, there was a long, awkward silence.

Then Lindsay turned to me and said, "So, Steve, Garrett tells me you're a marketing assistant now. What is that exactly?"

"What is it?" I said, shrugging, looking out at the canyon in the distance. "I don't know, Lindsay. To be perfectly honest, I have no idea."

"Do you think you'll stick with it?" she said.

"Who knows?" I said. "All of my adult life, I've either been a student or worked for a university, so I don't know where else I'd go."

"You should move out to California," Garrett said and smiled.

"Why?"

"I don't know." He shrugged. "California's great."

Sometime later, maybe around one or two in the morning, long after it had become clear that Paul and Elaine wouldn't be returning to join us, I walked over to the pool and found Garrett, who was sitting on the concrete edge, his blue jeans rolled up, his bare legs dangling loosely into the water. He was smoking a cigarette, which Paul had apparently given to him earlier.

"Can you believe he still keeps these things around?" he said, holding up the cigarette. "I told him to only give me one or I'd smoke the whole pack."

He held up the cigarette to me and I took a drag and then sat down beside him at the edge of the pool, taking off my shoes and rolling up my pants, and then putting my feet in the water, which was cold, but felt good. On the other side of the patio area, beside the table, Lindsay was talking to Amy, the two of them laughing like old friends.

"Any sign of them ever coming down?" Garrett said. "Paul and Elaine?"

"I don't know," I said. "I don't think so. I think they're probably done for the night."

He nodded. "I feel terrible about bringing up that study," he said.

"I wouldn't worry about it," I said. "I think they probably just had a little too much to drink, you know?"

He nodded again and then he moved his legs around in the water as I passed him the cigarette. "You know," he said, "what I didn't mention earlier, when we were talking about kids, was that one of the best parts about having kids is that you stop caring so much, you know?" He looked at me. "Before I had kids, all I used to care about was my career—it was really all I thought about—and it made me so miserable. Now I could care less. All that little stuff, you know, the petty stuff—the department politics and all that—you forget about it." He looked out at the lights in the canyon, and then he turned to me, as if realizing what he'd said. "I'm sorry," he said. "I didn't mean—"

"Don't worry about it," I said. Then I picked up the wineglass I'd been holding and took a sip. "Paul probably told you what happened to me, right?"

"Not the whole story," Garrett said. "But enough."

I nodded. "Did he tell you what he did?"

"What do you mean?"

I looked out at the canyon then and realized that I was probably drunk myself. "Did he tell you how he screwed me over?" I said.

Garrett looked at me. "What are you talking about?"

"Never mind," I said, and put down my glass.

"Look," he said. "I don't know what you think you know. But I can promise you Paul didn't screw you over. If anything, it was the opposite."

"What are you talking about?" I said, and then I told him about the split vote, about how obvious it had been that Paul had voted against me, about that night at our apartment when it had seemed so transparent.

Garrett nodded. Then he took a long drag on his cigarette and exhaled slowly. "Steve," he said, "I don't know what to tell you, but that's not Paul. He wouldn't do that." He paused. "Let me ask you something, though. Let's say he did do that, okay. Let's say all of that was true. Do you think it would've mattered anyway?"

"What do you mean?"

"I mean you would have still had to go through the university's tenure committee, the vice president, the president. There are a lot of other steps to the process, right? Do you think Paul's vote would have really made a difference?"

"That's not the point."

"It is, though," he said. "Kind of. Isn't it?"

I looked away.

"And for what it's worth," he said, "I know for a fact he went to the mat for you, Steve. He really did. You just hadn't published enough. It was out of his hands."

I looked at him. "What about the numbers, though? I missed a favorable vote by one person."

"What about them?" he said. "You know they always toy with the numbers to lessen the blow."

"Lessen the blow?"

"Yeah, you know . . ." He looked at me.

I turned out toward the canyon then and felt suddenly numb. I closed my eyes and felt something pass over me, something dark. I could hear Amy and Lindsay still laughing.

"I'm sorry," he said. "I probably shouldn't even be telling you this. In fact, I know I shouldn't be." He shook his head. "This is what happens when you drink all day. You start saying things you shouldn't."

"It's okay," I said, and then I picked up my wineglass and took a long sip. "It's fine."

Sometime shortly after that, Paul appeared at the top of the hill with his arm around Elaine. He was shouting something down to us, something about dessert, and beckoning us to come up the hill to join them. Garrett turned to me and shrugged. "Looks like they're still up," he said. Then he waved to Lindsay, and then a moment later the two of them were walking up the lit path toward the house, their arms linked.

I'd expected Amy to follow, but she didn't. Instead she walked over to me and sat down beside me on the concrete edge of the pool. We both turned around and waved up to Paul to let him know that we'd be up in a minute, and then he gave us the thumbs-up and started down the lit path toward Lindsay and Garrett.

Once they had all disappeared inside the house, Amy turned back to me and smiled, and then she rested her head on my shoulder.

"I'm pretty drunk," she said.

"Me too."

"You know I didn't mean to put you on the spot back there," she said. "About the kid stuff."

"It's okay," I said. "We haven't talked about it in a while. I kind of figured it was on your mind."

"You did?"

"Yeah."

She nodded. "So do you believe all that stuff they were saying about parenting and being miserable?"

"I don't know," I said. "I don't see how it could possibly matter anyway. If you want to have kids, you have kids, right?"

"Unless you can't."

"Right," I said, and glanced up at Paul and Elaine's house. "Unless you can't."

She looked at me. "You okay?"

"Yeah," I said. "I guess."

I looked up at the house where I could see Paul and Elaine and Garrett and Lindsay all standing on the back patio, beside a pair of Tiki torches, waving to us, and I thought about Paul and Elaine and how I'd stolen from them and how they probably had no idea that I had and how they might not even care anyway but how it somehow seemed important to me that they knew, important that I told them this or that I returned what I'd taken, though I knew I'd never do that. I had no idea whether the things that Garrett had just told me were true or not—they could have very easily been things that Paul had told him to make himself feel better—but at that moment I didn't care. At that moment, I simply felt worn out.

I looked back at Amy. "You know Garrett claims that Paul really did go to bat for me," I said. "It was just a hopeless cause."

"Oh yeah? And do you believe him?"

"I don't know," I said. "It's possible."

"Well, it's pointless to think about now, right?"

"I guess," I said, "though maybe he's right, you know? Maybe I could have done more to protect myself. Published more."

Amy shrugged. "You can't keep doing this to yourself, Steve."

"I know," I said, and then I picked up my glass, and Amy moved her legs around and stared out at the canyon.

"I'm serious," she said. "This can't be the rest of our lives, okay?"

I nodded.

Paul and Elaine and Garrett and Lindsay were now shouting something down to us from the top of the hill, though I couldn't make out what they were saying. I could only see their silhouettes moving back and forth in front of the lit patio door, holding up bowls and spoons, beckoning us to join them. Amy turned to me and shrugged.

"Should we go up to the house now?"

I shook my head, and then I pulled my legs out of the pool and began to put on my sandals.

"Let's go home," I said, and Amy nodded, and a moment later we started through the dark toward our car. I realized that this would probably be one of the last times we'd ever come here, one of the last times we'd ever see this amazing view—I don't know how I knew that then, but I did, I felt it—and as we walked back toward our car, I could hear Paul and Elaine, still standing at the top of the hill, shouting down to us, *Hey, come back!*, and then later, almost as if it were a chant or a prayer, the faint sound of their voices floating up and into the air behind us, then rising higher. *Dessert,* they were shouting, *dessert, dessert, dessert.*

Heroes of the Alamo

When I was twenty-three and recently married, I worked for a few months as a visitor services associate at the Alamo, which means I basically just stood at the entrance and greeted people when they arrived, told them not to touch anything (especially the walls), and fielded questions about the mission, its history, and the programming and activities available on-site. From time to time, I'd be called upon to do other things—for example, to show the orientation film or to man the queue outside the theater—but mostly I just stood at the entrance and tried to look friendly, tried to be helpful. "You're the Alamo's first ambassador," my supervisor, Glen, had told me the day they hired me. "That's not a small thing."

In the evenings after work, I'd meet my wife, Kayla, for drinks at an icehouse just south of downtown—an outdoor bar that served these two-dollar Tecates and Modelos during happy hour and that sold the most incredible empanadas out of an old food truck that sat parked perpetually at the back of the property. Kayla had just started her first grown-up job as a junior architect at a firm downtown and always showed up in her work clothes, sweating and cursing the heat. Sometimes she'd change into a T-shirt and skirt in the icehouse bathroom, but usually she'd just endure it, drinking the cold beers until she no longer felt hot.

Out along the periphery of the property were these gorgeous flowering vines and creosote bushes, wild bougainvillea and lavender. The air at that icehouse always smelled of hibiscus, I remember, and they usually played a lot of old Mexican standards from the thirties and forties on the stereo, acoustic versions of songs like "La Martiniana" and "La Llorona" and "Naila." Sometimes we'd call up our friends and ask them to join us, but most nights we just hung out alone, the two of us, talking about our days and our uncertain futures, about the endless possibilities that lay before us, sipping on cold Modelos with lime, feasting on the endless supply of free chips.

Anyway, at some point in the summer—I can't remember when exactly—we started to play this game called "Heroes of the Alamo." I can't recall precisely how this came about—it must have been Kayla's idea—but it would usually happen after we'd both had a few beers and the sun had gone down at the far end of the property and the regulars had begun to show, the whole atmosphere of the icehouse getting livelier. Kayla was well aware of how bored I got during the slow stretches at my job—I complained about this often—and I had told her recently about how I'd begun to memorize the names on the plaques arranged around the main room, the names of the numerous soldiers who had died there. I can't remember now why I even mentioned this to her, but Kayla had found it strangely endearing and liked to listen to me as I recited them. If I could recite more than twenty, she'd told me the first time I'd mentioned it, she'd buy the next round. Then it became forty, then fifty, until eventually we got close to a hundred. There was no way I was ever going to be able to memorize all of the deceased—there were simply too many, and my memory wasn't that great—but the more names I learned the more it seemed to please Kayla.

"Come on," she'd sometimes beg when friends would show up. "Show them."

And I'd look down, embarrassed at first, then reluctantly begin.

"Well, Davy Crockett, of course," I'd say. "William Barrett Travis. James Bowie."

"Micajah Autry," she might add, egging me on.

"That's right, Micajah Autry."

And on we'd go.

Sometimes our friends would smile nervously, not sure if they were supposed to find this amusing or not; other times, they'd simply applaud loudly or feign amazement, but most of the time, they'd just look kind of puzzled and embarrassed, as if they'd been let in on an inside joke they didn't quite get.

And, to be honest, I wasn't quite sure I got it myself. I wasn't quite sure why Kayla enjoyed it so much, what it meant to her.

All I know is that as the summer went on, and as we moved into fall, the weather getting cooler now, the game began to take on a different feel, a sadder feel, the slow dirge-like tone of a requiem, or an elegy, a lament for all of the soldiers who had died there, all of those faceless names I'd been reciting and internalizing for the past few months. All of that *death*. After a while, it began to bother me, the heaviness of it, the heaviness of the game itself, and one evening I remember feeling so overcome with sadness, I simply stopped reciting.

"Why did you stop?" Kayla said.

"I don't think I like this anymore," I said.

"Why not?"

"I don't know."

It was a cold night and the icehouse lot was mostly empty, just a few diehards bundled in wool jackets and scarves, sitting at picnic tables, nursing their beers. The leaves had fallen from the trees and the festive lights of summer had been replaced with Halloween decorations and painted masks for Día de los Muertos.

Kayla looked at me. In a month from now she'd get an offer from a firm in Seattle that would simply be too good to pass up—it was a "career maker" was how she put it—and that departure—what we called at first a six-month experiment, then a long-distance inconvenience, and finally a trial separation—would mark the beginning of the end of our marriage.

But all of that was still far away from my thoughts that night. That night I was still trying to channel the lightness of those early days of summer, when we didn't have to fill the lulls in our conversations with games, when we didn't have to be out drinking to be able to talk to each other.

Kayla reached across the table and took my hand. "We don't have to do it anymore," she said. "Why don't we go home?"

And I nodded, and we stood up, and paid our bill, and then started on the long walk home to our apartment in King William, our bodies braced against the sudden wind, our shoulders turned downward and stiff, our footsteps moving silently in a quiet and steady cadence, as if we were marching in a funeral or a wedding or a war.

Bees

They arrived in late April.

According to the beekeeper we'd brought out to the house, they'd found a way into our laundry room wall and had been building a hive in there for some time. Our laundry room is attached to our garage—it's a separate outdoor structure, removed from the main house by about twenty yards—and that's where they'd decided to build their home.

My wife, Alexis, was the one who first noticed them, circling in a small cloud near the back fence of our yard, right next to the laundry room window. When she got stung a few days later, taking a small basket of hand towels and dishcloths out to the laundry room, we called up the beekeeper and had him come out and take a look. Apparently, there are a lot of people out there who will remove your bees for free, bee enthusiasts, I guess—or maybe bee conservationists is a better term—but Alexis didn't want to take any chances. She wanted a professional, or a team of professionals, if need be.

As it turned out, the guy we hired was able to remove the bees in a fairly humane way—taking out a part of the drywall, then using this vacuum device to suck the bees into a large wood box, which he then transported to another part of the county, some part of the Hill Country outside of San Antonio, where, he assured us, the bees would prosper.

Before he left, he reminded us that we'd want to have the honeycomb removed from the inside of the wall within the next few months—bees have an excellent sense of smell, he said, and a new swarm would very likely return next spring if we didn't have the honeycomb removed. He also suggested having the insides of the walls thoroughly cleaned and scrubbed down, filled with insulation, then carefully sealed up. The cost of doing that would be expensive, he said, but it was a necessary precaution.

As I followed him out to his truck, parked in front of our house, I thanked him again and told him we'd be in touch in a couple months about the other stuff.

"We'd do it now," I said, handing him the check, "only it's not the best time."

"Sure," he said, without looking at me, as if he'd somehow intuited what I was referring to. "Just let us know."

The reason it wasn't the best time was that we had just begun what Alexis was now referring to as our trial separation. She'd moved into an apartment downtown, closer to her job, and during the week she sometimes slept there in the evenings. For the time being, our daughter, Rhea, was staying with me. We'd told Rhea, who is five, that sometimes her mother had to stay downtown for work—that she sometimes had to sleep there when it got too late to come home— and so far Rhea, who is a very bright and perceptive child, hadn't questioned it.

In the evenings, whenever Alexis was home, we carried on in much the same way as we had before. We ate dinner together, watched TV, spent the late evenings talking about Rhea's schedule, planning her play dates, covering our credit card bills. The only real difference was that sometimes Alexis would leave at the end of the evening, after Rhea had gone to sleep, or other times never show up at all. Personally, I didn't really know what this separation meant. Alexis had assured me that she had no intention of divorcing me. She said that she was doing this to strengthen our marriage, to strengthen herself. She'd fallen into a pretty dark place lately, she said, and now she was trying her best to get out of it. This time alone—whatever she did downtown in the evenings—was somehow helping.

I'd known about Alexis's dark places before we ever married. She'd been prone to depression even in college, when we'd met, twelve years earlier, and had been on any number of antidepressants over the years. She went to therapy about as often as most people go to the gym, but she hadn't suffered any type of postpartum depression after Rhea's birth and had been more or less okay for the first few years of Rhea's life. It was only in the past year or so that I'd noticed a change, some of her old anxieties coming back—a fear of social engagements, a preoccupation with Rhea's health and her own. She'd started smoking again during the Christmas holiday, and that's when I knew that something had happened. She hadn't smoked a cigarette since college.

When I asked her about it one night in late January, as we were sitting out on the back deck of our house after dinner, Rhea watching a show inside, Alexis just drew on her cigarette and shrugged. "It's really fucked up, I know. I stress about my health all the time, right, but the only way I can settle down my fear of dying is by smoking."

"I'm not talking about the smoking," I said. "I'm talking about everything."

She nodded. And that was the first time she brought it up—the apartment. That was the first time she mentioned it.

What I hadn't been able to explain to the beekeeper was that the reason we hadn't been able to afford to have the honeycomb removed from the inside of our laundry room wall was that the cost of Alexis's apartment had spread us so thin financially that we could barely afford to cover Rhea's day care. We were managing, but barely. It wasn't a tenable long-term situation. We didn't talk about this very much, but that evening, when I came in from talking to the bee-keeper, I felt inclined to mention it.

"We don't have to get the thing removed immediately," I said, "but we don't want to wait too long either. If we do, they'll be back. Or another swarm will move in, and that could be worse."

She nodded.

"Nothing's sealed, is what I'm saying," I continued, and then I sat down at the table and watched her as she packed up her bag for the evening. Before the beekeeper came, she'd talked about making dinner when Rhea got home from her play date next door, but now I could see that she'd changed her mind.

"Will you be back tomorrow?" I said.

"What's tomorrow?"

"Saturday. Rhea has soccer."

"It's Friday already?"

"Didn't anyone mention that at work?"

"I didn't go to work today."

"Why not?"

"I have vacation saved up." She looked at me. There was a defensiveness in her tone, so I didn't push.

Outside the window, I could see that the cloud of bees was virtually gone, just a few stragglers, which we'd been told to expect.

"Whatever," I said, smiling, taking her hand. "Just let us know."

On the nights when Alexis appeared and then disappeared, it was harder for Rhea. I knew that she could sense that something was going on, that it didn't make sense for her mother to be home for dinner, but then not stay for her bedtime routine, or that she'd be home after school to play with her, but then not stay for dinner.

That night, when Rhea came back from her play date next door, we had our typical Friday night ritual—the movie *Frozen*, followed by ice cream—but she didn't say a word about her mother. She didn't ask me where she was or why she hadn't stayed for dinner or when she would be coming back, all of which was very unusual. Later, as I was tucking her into bed, I asked her if there was anything she wanted to talk about.

"Like what?"

"Like your mother?"

"Mommy's in heaven."

I stared at her. "Your mother's downtown. She's not in heaven."

"That's what I meant," she said. Then she closed her eyes.

Was she messing with me? Kids say all sorts of strange stuff, but this felt calculated.

"You know, Mommy's coming to soccer tomorrow," I said. Alexis hadn't actually agreed to this, but I now felt worried enough to text her.

Rhea said nothing.

"Did you hear what I just said?"

Rhea kept her eyes closed. "I'm sleeping, Daddy."

"Did you hear what I just said about your mother?"

She was quiet for a long time, and then, finally, she opened her eyes and looked at me. "Yes," she said. "I heard."

The next morning I sent Alexis a text asking her to come to Rhea's soccer practice. I didn't mention anything about what Rhea had said, but I'd written in all caps that it was very important that she come.

Alexis had written back, *Ok. Will try to.*

Please, I wrote a few minutes later. *Very important.*

This time she didn't respond, which I took as a bad sign.

I went into Rhea's room and woke her up, made her breakfast, started straightening up the house. I looked out the window and saw that several of our trees were dying.

I needed help, but I didn't know who to ask. I couldn't ask my mother. She already had her problems with Alexis, and if I told her about the apartment thing, that would be it. I had my brother, Cal, up in Austin, but he could come down only so often, and usually only for a few hours at a time. I had various friends with kids, but it somehow felt like a betrayal to Alexis to let them in on what was happening. If I did, it was probably unlikely that we'd ever be able to hang out with them again in a normal way. So what could I do? It seemed like I had a number of vague possibilities but no real options.

I was thinking about this later that day, as I drove out to the junior high near our house where Rhea had her weekly soccer practice. It was hot, easily a hundred degrees, by the time we arrived at the field. Rhea had said very little that morning, and I had hopes that we'd see Alexis's car in the parking lot when we arrived, but it wasn't there.

I didn't say anything about this, and neither did Rhea.

As Rhea's soccer coach lined the kids up in front of a row of orange cones, I stood in the shade of a live oak and texted Alexis again.

We need to talk, I wrote.

But, again, I heard nothing.

We need to talk, I wrote one more time, *soon*.

At first, the situation with the apartment had seemed reasonable. I knew how it might look to people on the outside, but it seemed reasonable to me, and I knew that Alexis wouldn't take advantage of it, which she didn't. She only used the apartment when she absolutely needed to, maybe one or two nights a week.

Lately, though, those one or two nights a week had turned into three or four, and sometimes five. I knew that I was partially to blame for this, that I had allowed it to happen out of fear, but I also didn't feel like I had much of a choice. Our household was in a tenuous position. If I pushed too hard, it might all collapse.

Still, this thing that Rhea had said the night before—this thing about Alexis being in heaven—it had unsettled me, and on the drive home from soccer practice that day, I sent Alexis another text, asking her to please call me as soon as she could. And then, when we got home, I called her up and left a message on her voicemail, explaining that I was very worried about Rhea and how all of this time away might be affecting her.

I was standing out on the back deck of the house as I did this, and Rhea was inside watching a show. It was late afternoon and very humid. Over by the laundry room window, I could see that there were still a number of bees, more than there had been that morning, more than a few stragglers.

After I'd finished my message to Alexis, I called the beekeeper and told him what was happening, but he said that this was all very normal, to just give it a few days. If they weren't gone in a few days, he said, he'd come back and take care of it.

I went back inside and grabbed a beer from the fridge, then headed back out to the deck. I sat in the shade and drank my beer and watched the bees.

After dinner, Alexis called. She said that she'd spent the day exercising and reading a book, a book that was helping her to center herself. It was a little "New Agey," she said, but still pretty good. She said she felt terrible about missing Rhea's soccer practice and hoped it went well.

I'd been prepared to confront her about all of the stuff I'd alluded to in my message, but somehow I lost my nerve. Instead, I just told her I was happy she was feeling better.

"I know that none of this is fair to you," she said at one point.

"It's fine," I said.

"And I know it's not fair to Rhea."

I said nothing.

"It's not like I'm not making progress, though. Some days are just better than others."

"I know."

She said a little bit more about the book she was reading, but I was only half-listening. When we hung up, I felt terrible.

I thought about calling her back, but instead went in search of Rhea, who was lying on the floor in her bedroom, drawing.

"Who were you talking to?" she said when she noticed me in the doorway.

"No one," I said.

She looked at me. "Do you think we can do a song tonight?"

"A song? Sure."

"My choice?"

"If you want."

This was something we'd started doing together a few months earlier. I'd read about it in a book. The book said that it was a good idea to try to expose your child to things that were important to you, that this was as important to them as it was to you, and so I'd started introducing Rhea to some of the music I liked, mostly music I'd liked when I was younger—Joy Division, The Smiths, Echo and the Bunnymen, those types of bands.

She seemed to like the music I played for her. Sometimes I couldn't tell if she really liked it or if she just said she did to spare my feelings. The one song I was certain she liked, though, was the song "Thirteen," by Big Star. For a whole week she made me play it for her every night before she went to sleep. I liked the original but she preferred a cover by Elliott Smith, which was kind of low production, very spare and haunting. I didn't mention to her that Elliott Smith had taken his own life when he was thirty-four. Like all the stuff that was going on with her mother, it wasn't something I felt she needed to know.

That night, after we'd listened to a few songs by the Velvet Underground, she asked me if I would play "Thirteen" for her again.

"Do you know what this song is about?" I said.

"It's about us."

"Us?"

"Like when you pick me up at school, or when we go to the pool."

I didn't have the heart to correct her in the way my own father would have corrected me. If that's what the song meant to her, that's what it meant. Who was I to ruin it?

She came over to me and sat on my lap and closed her eyes, and I held her.

Later that night, after she'd fallen asleep, I went out to the kitchen and poured myself a beer. I saw that Alexis had sent me a text. There wasn't any writing on it, though. Just a photo of the view from her downtown apartment: a few trees at the edge of a park, some buildings behind, a fountain. I thought of writing back to her about the view but realized I had nothing to say. Finally, I just wrote good night, and then turned over the phone and went to bed.

The next morning when I got up, Rhea was already sitting at the kitchen table eating a breakfast bar and drinking from her sippy cup, her eyes focused on her iPad. I reminded her of our new rule—no watching shows while she was eating—but she said she wasn't watching a show, she was talking to her mother. I walked over to the iPad and looked, but the screen was blank. I knew that they sometimes did video chats, especially when Alexis was staying downtown, but this seemed early in the day for that type of thing.

"Are you telling me the truth?" I said.

Rhea nodded.

"What were you and Mommy talking about?"

"Heaven."

I looked at her. "You need to stop that."

"What?"

"Seriously," I said. "I don't want you saying stuff like that anymore."

She looked down.

I picked up the iPad, took it over to the closet next to the refrigerator, and placed it up on one of the highest shelves, far from her reach. Rhea started crying.

"You can have it back after lunch," I said, "but not this morning."

She got up from the table and ran to her room. I knew she didn't understand what she'd done, or maybe she did but didn't understand why she was being punished for it.

I walked over to the counter and started my coffee, and then I checked my phone, but there were no new messages from Alexis. No new texts either. This was the first time she'd stayed away both Friday and Saturday night, and I felt like things were slipping away from me. I wrote her a brief text asking if she could meet us somewhere for lunch. It was fine if she wasn't ready to come home yet, I wrote, but it would be nice to see her.

Later, as I stood at the sink, cleaning up the breakfast dishes, I thought about some of the strange things she'd been saying to me lately, comments about not knowing how much longer she could continue working at her job or whether she could ever really talk to her parents again. I didn't really know how to respond to these things. They seemed to come out of nowhere, like a lot of the stuff she'd been saying in the past month, so I just shrugged and reminded her what quitting her job would do to us. Not only would she have to give up the apartment, but it would basically mean the end of Rhea's day care, not to mention a major hit to our mortgage and our monthly expenses. It worried me that she might just go ahead and do it anyway, though, without mentioning it to me, just like she'd done with the apartment. It seemed like something that might happen.

In the other room, I could hear Rhea turning on some music—her Disney songs, not the music I'd introduced her to—so I took my coffee out to the back deck and tried to get my thoughts together, tried to figure out what we might do that day.

In the distance, I could see that our neighbor was working on the bushes in his backyard, spraying them with some type of pesticide. I looked back at the laundry room and saw that the bee situation was even worse. Not only were there about twice as many bees now, but there was also something else—a small hole at the base of the laundry room wall that the bees seemed to be entering and exiting in large numbers.

I put down my coffee and headed over there to check it out, standing at the far edge of the swarm, being sure to keep a safe distance, even though the beekeeper had assured me these types of bees weren't aggressive.

From what I could tell, it looked like a small animal of some sort, maybe a raccoon or a possum, had chewed through the wood completely—the beekeeper had mentioned this could happen—making a small hole in the wall, no bigger than a softball, and then burrowing inside to get the honeycomb, which was now lying in the grass, completely devoid of honey.

I called the beekeeper, even though it was a Sunday morning, and left a long message describing what I was looking at: the small hole, the bees crawling in and out of it in large numbers, the empty honeycomb lying on the grass beside it.

After that, I called Alexis and described the same thing. Then, just as I was hanging up the phone, just as I was turning around and heading back inside, I felt something at the back of my head, right behind my ear, a faint rustling in my hair, a buzzing, and then as I was reaching back to swat it, a sharp sting on the side of my neck, a sharp needling sensation that was shocking mainly for how painful it was. A moment later, more bees were swarming around my head—it seemed like close to fifty—and I was running back to the house, getting stung once more, again on my neck, before reaching the back door.

Inside, I found Rhea lying on the couch in her pajamas, drawing in her coloring book.

I told her to get dressed.

"Where are we going?"

"Downtown," I said, "to get your mother."

I didn't actually know the address of Alexis's apartment. I'd never been there before, and she had never given it to me. She'd wanted to keep it a secret, I guess. But based on the photos she'd sent me I had a rough idea of where it was. I knew the park, for example, and recognized one of the buildings as being a hotel where we'd once gone for a formal event.

On the way down, I called her voicemail again, telling her that we were on our way, that we were coming to get her, that we needed to talk. If I had had more time to think about it, I probably would have taken a different approach—we had agreed never to mention the apartment to Rhea, for example, and now I was taking her there—but the pain in the back of my head was worse, it was throbbing now, and the area around the side of my neck where I'd been stung was starting to swell up. It was hard to think of anything else.

In the backseat, Rhea was sitting quietly, not saying a word. As we passed the children's museum, where she always begged me to take her, I turned on the radio and tried my best to find a station she might like. I could feel my neck still swelling, a warmth now spreading across the skin above my shoulders.

Later, when we pulled up to the park that I'd recognized from Alexis's photo the night before, I parked the car and looked back at Rhea. She was just staring at me, blank-faced. I asked her if she was hungry and she shook her head. *Are you sure?* She nodded. A moment later, Alexis called, upset.

"What are you doing?" she said.

"We're here," I said.

"Where?"

"Outside. By the park."

"You brought Rhea? What are you thinking?"

"We need to talk."

"You're just going to confuse her."

"It's the bee situation," I said. "It's worse."

She was quiet for a long time.

"It's just not a good time for me," she said finally. "Can we do this tomorrow?"

"One hour."

She was quiet again. Then she said, "I'll meet you at Zinc. Twenty minutes. It's right around the corner."

At an earlier time in our lives, Alexis and I used to go to this café all the time—The Zinc Café—but as I sat there now with Rhea, sipping on a beer, pressing a cube of ice against the side of my neck, I realized we hadn't been there together in close to seven years.

Rhea was coloring on her menu, and in the small courtyard outside the dark restaurant, people were sitting under umbrellas beside the River Walk, sipping on wine and mojitos, eating chips and guacamole in the sweltering heat.

Inside, the restaurant was virtually empty, and in the half hour since we'd been here Rhea had twice asked me to take her home. "It's so cold in here," she'd said, "and dark. And strange." Now she was staring at me, concerned.

"It's worse, Daddy," she said.

"What?"

"Your neck. It's more swollen." She narrowed her eyes like a worried doctor.

"I'll be fine," I said, though I was wondering now if I might be allergic. I hadn't been stung by a bee since I was a kid.

"You should go see Dr. Ritvo," she said.

"Dr. Ritvo is a children's doctor."

"He could help you."

When the waitress passed, I ordered another beer and Rhea looked at me again, bit her lip, then looked out the window.

"I want to go home," she said, now for the third time.

"Just give her a few more minutes."

"She's not coming."

"You don't know that."

"Yes," she said, looking out the window. "I do."

At home that night, I made us frozen pizzas and let Rhea watch a cartoon while she ate. I could tell that the day's events had rattled her. Earlier, when we'd pulled into the driveway, bees had surrounded the car, and she'd started to cry. She'd refused to get out. Now, every time she noticed one close to the kitchen window, she'd scream that they were coming in.

I was sitting on the couch with a big bag full of ice cubes pressed against my neck. I'd taken some Benadryl earlier, but the swelling was still pretty bad. I looked out the window and saw that the swarm of bees was probably about twice as big as it had been that morning, possibly growing. After Rhea had finished her pizza, I stood up and went into the kitchen and pulled down the iPad from the high shelf where I'd hidden it, and then I began to search through it for the playlist I'd made for her earlier in the week, a playlist of all of her favorite songs from the past month or so as well as a few Elliott Smith songs that I thought she might like.

Once I found it, I told her to come over and have a seat on the couch next to me, but she said she didn't feel like listening to any music tonight. She just wanted to be alone.

I looked down at my cell phone. In the two hours since we'd been home, Alexis hadn't called once, hadn't made any attempt to contact us at all since flaking out on us at Zinc. I turned over the phone and looked back at Rhea.

"Come on," I said. "I made something for you."

"What?" she asked, and came over gradually, her eyes full of skepticism.

"It's just a few songs I think you'll like," I said, and then I cleared the blankets on the couch away, so that she could sit down next to me.

Later that night, after Rhea had fallen asleep beside me on the couch, I had a memory of something Alexis had said to me earlier in our marriage. This was just after we'd moved into our first apartment in San Antonio, before we'd ever talked about buying a house or having children. She'd been fired from her job at a radio station downtown and had come home that night, drunk and very angry. She'd gone out with some of her coworkers after getting the bad news, and they'd bought her shot after shot, and then put her in a cab and sent her back to me, and before I'd even had a chance to ask her what had happened, she'd gone into the bathroom and smashed the mirror with her fist, and then come back out, screaming her head off, blood dripping all over the carpet. I ran into the kitchen and grabbed some dish towels and tried my best to stop the bleeding and calm her down, but she was laughing now, not screaming, but laughing, and trying to pull me toward her, trying to kiss me.

"You're drunk," I said, pushing her off. "And hurt."

"I'm not that drunk," she said, and then she cupped my face in her hands and stared at me so intently it felt like she was seeing inside me.

"I know you like it," she said.

"What?"

"This," she said, smiling. "I know this is why you married me. You like it."

I pushed her away then and went into the kitchen to get her some water, but the memory of that moment had always stayed with me. It was like she'd hit on some shameful secret between us that we never spoke about: that I was attracted to the part of her that also scared me the most.

I was thinking about this later that night as I sat in the family room with Rhea, staring out the sliding glass doors at the bees in our backyard, listening to the playlist I'd made for her.

Outside, it was almost dark, and it was getting hard to discern the swarm of bees against the blackening sky, though I knew that they were out there somewhere, in the distance. It was just hard to know where. I reached down and touched Rhea's shoulder and pulled her closer. Then I picked up the phone and called Alexis again, knowing she probably wouldn't answer, hoping she would. The phone rang a few times, but no answer. I called again, same thing. I thought of leaving her a message, but instead tried one last time, and this time she actually picked up, her voice soft and distant now, dreamy, like she'd just woken up. I asked her if I'd woken her, but she said I hadn't. She said she'd just been reading a book.

"How are you?" I said.

"I'm okay," she said. "Tired. I'm sorry about earlier."

"It's okay."

"I just wasn't expecting you guys."

"I know," I said.

She was quiet for a long time. Then she said, "I need a few more days, I think."

"A few more days? What about work?"

"I'm taking my vacation."

I bit my lip. "I think you need to come home."

She was quiet.

"Okay," I said. "A few more days. But definitely in a few more days, right?"

"I don't know."

I had to restrain myself. I knew if I pushed I'd lose her.

"I need something a little more definite here."

"I know," she said, "and if I could give you something a little more definite, I would."

"This is crazy."

"What?"

"Are you ever coming home?

"What's that supposed to mean?"

"Are you ever coming home?"

She was silent.

"That wasn't actually a serious question," I said, but she didn't respond.

I could hear the sound of cars beeping on the street outside her apartment, music playing on the TV, and I felt the warmth again on the side of my neck, the throbbing.

"We just want to see you," I said finally. "Rhea especially."

"I know that," she said. "I know that you do."

After we hung up, I put down the phone and put my arm around Rhea and pulled her close again. In the background, I could hear the words of her favorite song playing, Elliott Smith's whispery voice, and I suddenly felt it, that we were entering into another phase, a deeper phase, a phase without any foreseeable end. I braced myself. In the distance, at the far end of the yard, it was completely dark now, though I knew that they were back there somewhere, in the darkness, circling the laundry room wall, swirling in slow motions, probably growing in number.

Pozole

That winter I went there every single day for lunch and ordered the same thing: pozole soup. I was forty-three years old. My second child had just been born. I had very little else in my life that I considered my own. These little lunches were my secret. The restaurant itself was nothing fancy, just a little hole-in-the-wall on the south side of San Antonio. During the lunch hour, it was mostly empty, but those in the know knew. They knew about the soup, and there were several like myself who went there regularly, just for the pozole.

We'd sit at the far end of the bar by ourselves, solemn as parishioners, eating our soup, never once looking at each other, certainly never talking. When we finished, we'd pay our checks and leave.

It got to the point where I didn't even have to order anymore. The bartenders knew me, and they knew why I was there. When they saw me appear at the end of the bar, they'd simply smile, nod, and put in my order. A few minutes later, I'd be presented with a fresh bowl of pozole.

In the world outside of this restaurant, my life was chaos. With two young children at home, my wife and I rarely slept, rarely even spoke to each other anymore. But when I was here, in this restaurant, all of that was gone. I had my forty-five minutes alone with my soup and my newspaper and, every once in a while, a glass of wine. The restaurant itself was dark, but in a calming way, and the music they played was usually light and acoustic Mexican music, older songs from the thirties and forties. The clientele was mostly older, too, or so it seemed, people who had probably been coming to this place for twenty or thirty years. I remember one older woman who always sat by herself at the far end of the bar and talked with one of the older bartenders. I had figured that they must be friends, or maybe even involved romantically, and that's why she came here each day. But then that bartender was fired, or stopped working there, and I realized my mistake. It hadn't been about the companionship at all. Like the rest of us, she'd only been coming for the soup.

Anyway, at some point—I can't remember why—my schedule changed, and I had to give up my lunches for a while. When I returned, a couple of months later, the restaurant looked different. The lighting was brighter and the walls had been painted beige. Also, all of the old photographs behind the bar had been removed. I asked the bartender what had happened, and he shrugged and said, "New ownership."

I then looked at the menu and saw that this, too, had been changed. It was glossy now, and much more colorful, and under *Soups* it only said *Tortilla*. "No more pozole?" I said, and I'm pretty sure my voice cracked.

He simply stared at me plaintively. "It was the owner's wife's recipe," he said. "It wasn't negotiable."

The restaurant was much livelier than usual, and I could tell that business had probably picked up since the change, but still, something was missing, too. The old clientele was no longer there. The diehards at the end of the bar, ladling soup into their mouths. Where had they gone?

"Is there another place," I began. "I mean, do you know . . ."

But then I stopped myself because both of us knew that there was no other place in the city where I would find a bowl of pozole soup like that.

Jimena

1.

The story of Jimena always changes.

Sometimes she's the woman my wife left me for; other times she's the woman I left my wife for; other times still, she's neither of those things.

I don't talk about Jimena very much anymore and neither does my wife, Carly. I never left my wife, and she never left me, but in a sense this isn't exactly true, either.

When Jimena came into our lives, we were both thirty-eight years old, and recently married. Prior to this we had dated and lived together for close to ten years. Jimena lived in the apartment below ours, but we didn't actually meet her until she had lived there almost six months. We were aware of her, of course—a lean, attractive woman in her late twenties who seemed to slip in and out of her apartment at odd times, late at night or in the early hours of the morning, but we never actually spoke to her.

I remember listening to the sound of Jimena coming home late at night with groups of her friends, or sometimes a boyfriend, stumbling into furniture, knocking over table lamps, always laughing. She drank a lot back then, went out four or five nights a week. I had no idea whether or not she had a job, but I assumed that she must.

"She's still living like she's twenty-one," Carly said to me one night as we were lying in bed, listening to the sound of Jimena walking around her apartment downstairs drunkenly.

"Maybe she's younger than we think," I said.

"Maybe," she said. "But she's not twenty-one."

Carly disapproved of Jimena, had disapproved of her from almost the get-go. Later, Jimena would laugh about this—the way that Carly used to "ice" her in the hallways whenever she passed, shooting her nasty looks or other times just ignoring her altogether. "She thought I was a prostitute, I think," Jimena once said with a laugh, "or maybe just a drug addict." Jimena was of course neither of those things. She was an art student at the Southwest School of Art, earning a BFA in ceramics. She worked in the mornings at a bakery in our neighborhood on the south side of San Antonio and spent her afternoons in class or putting in long hours at the studio. In the evenings, she went out, usually with friends, but sometimes alone. She told me all of this over coffee one morning when she showed up at our door, unannounced, locked out of her apartment again.

This had been happening to Jimena a lot lately. She apparently had a door that locked from the inside whenever she closed it, and she seemed to forget this fact often. Usually I'd hear her wandering around the downstairs hallways, knocking on people's doors, asking if she could borrow a cell phone. That day, though, she'd run out of luck on the first floor and had started up the stairwell to the second. When I answered her knock, she looked both discouraged and annoyed.

"I asked them to change that lock," she said without introducing herself. "I ask them every week."

"Would you like to come in?" I said.

She stared at me.

"You could use my cell to call Benny." Benny was the off-site manager of our apartment building, an older man who was notorious for never answering his phone.

Jimena crossed her arms and continued to stare at me. I could tell she was sizing me up, deciding whether or not she could trust me.

"Or you could just call from right here," I said, pulling my phone out of my pocket, unlocking the home screen, and handing it to her.

She looked at the phone, and without saying anything took it down the hallway and dialed a number—I assumed Benny's—while looking out the large barred window at the far end of the hall. I stood in the doorway and watched her as she talked into the phone, her back still turned to me. She was wearing only a long black T-shirt, one that fell all the way to her knees, and her hair was wet, as if she'd just gotten out of the shower. She wasn't wearing shoes.

When she finished her call, she came back to me and handed me the phone.

"He said he'll be here in twenty minutes."

"Which means forty."

"Right." She smiled.

"Are you sure you don't want to come in?" I said. "I was just making coffee. You can use my laptop if you need to check email or anything."

Again she stared at me skeptically, shifting her weight from one foot to the other, but I guess in the end she must have decided I was harmless, or perhaps she didn't really care.

"Okay," she said finally, glancing around the hallway one last time. "Maybe just for a minute."

By the time Jimena left that day, I'd learned a lot about her. I'd learned that she'd grown up in Belize, that she'd lived in different parts of Mexico during her childhood, that she'd only moved to San Antonio in high school. I learned that she'd never known her father, that she had two sisters, both older, and that her mother still lived in Monterrey. She lived with an aunt, a cousin of her mother's, during high school, and then she'd lived for a while in California, though she didn't seem to like to talk about that time. "That was a really fucked-up period," she said at one point, waving her hand, and then added, as if it were an afterthought, "I was almost married." Since then, though, she'd been back in San Antonio and working hard on her BFA, trying to do what she should have been doing years ago: getting her degree. As for me, I said little about my own life, only that I was out of work at the moment but working on several projects, including a documentary film about some of the local artists on the south side of San Antonio. I rattled off a few names, figuring Jimena might have heard of them, but she hadn't.

"I don't really like to hang out with artists," she said. "Most of them are so self-involved."

I nodded.

"I just like to do my own thing, not talk about it."

I asked her what her own thing was, and she said sculpture.

"Any particular type?"

"Yeah." She smiled. "The good type."

. . .

Later that day, when Carly got home, I told her about my conversation with Jimena. Carly was working at the time as a publicist for a local arts organization and usually came home stressed and annoyed.

"Did she tell you her rate?" she said.

"She's not a prostitute," I said. "She's an art student actually."

"That's what all prostitutes say."

I gave her a look. "What's up with you?"

"I think I'm being replaced."

"By who?"

"The intern."

"The college student?"

"Yeah." She nodded. "Only she's not actually a college student. She's twenty-four." She pulled out a bottle of mescal from the cabinet above the sink and poured herself a small glass.

"Going straight for the strong stuff tonight, huh?"

"Tonight," she said. "Yes, I am."

Carly had been working for this arts organization for a little over five years. They'd already fired her once before, during the recession, citing cutbacks, then they'd hired her back eight months later, but ever since that time she'd been on edge about her employment status. She'd never been fired from anything in her life, and I could tell it had rattled her. We didn't talk about this much, but whenever she had a bad day at work, pissed someone off, or made a mistake, or whenever someone else did something well, she believed she was being replaced.

That night, as we lay in bed listening to the sound of Jimena and two of her friends playing music downstairs—some type of retro punk band, thick bass, heavy guitar—Carly leaned into me and held me tight.

"Doesn't she make you feel old sometimes?" she said.

"Who? Jimena?"

"Yeah," she said.

"No," I said. "Not really. And I don't know why you think about her so much. We barely know her."

"I know," she said and squeezed my arm. "I don't know why I think about her so much either."

When Carly and I first met, she was still working on her under-graduate degree in art history at UTSA. She'd taken off a few years to live in Southtown and work for a nonprofit organization that brought writers and artists into the public schools. She'd helped build that organization from the ground up and was sad to leave it, I think, was still uncertain if she wanted to be back in school at all. We were living on the south side then, and twice a week Carly would make the half hour commute up to the UTSA campus and take her classes, while I worked various part-time jobs in our neighborhood, mostly landscaping and carpentry jobs, jobs that I could pick up easily and that paid well enough to get us through the lean days at the end of the month.

She sometimes forgot this though—that there was a time when I was supporting her and not the other way around. When I got the inheritance from my grandfather a few years later—not a fortune, but enough to live on for a while, if we lived modestly—I stopped work-ing altogether. I'd been working at a television news station on the north side then, as a sound editor, but as soon as the money came through from my grandfather, I gave them my notice and left. I told Carly that I wanted to use the opportunity to pursue other projects, including the documentary film I was working on. That was almost five years ago, though, and Carly still said it was the worst thing that had ever happened to me—getting that money. The worst thing that had ever happened to *us*.

As for the documentary film I was working on at the time, it wasn't so much a project as a distraction from the fact that I had no idea what I wanted to be doing, or what I was supposed to be doing, with my life. It was also a convenient way of explaining to people at parties why I wasn't currently employed. I'd started the film a few years earlier but had made little progress to date. I'd interviewed over a dozen local artists since I'd started the process, yet could find no common thread, no unifying theme that gave the project focus. The last artist I'd interviewed was a muralist named Amaya Sotel, who lived a few blocks away from the apartment Carly and I used to live in before we lived in this one. That interview was one of the strangest and most awkward conversations I'd ever had in my life. At one point I'd wondered if Amaya Sotel was stoned, or perhaps on some type of hallucinogenic, like mescaline. It seemed like she wasn't even aware that I was in the room with her.

After that, I basically gave up on the project for a while, though I didn't tell Carly this, and it wasn't until I met Jimena that I'd even considered doing another interview for it.

In retrospect, I wonder whether I was simply using the interview as an excuse to talk to Jimena again or whether I genuinely believed that she might be the one to help me reboot my project. Either way, when I ran into her a few days later, coming into the apartment building just as I was going out, I asked her if she had a moment to talk. She looked at me skeptically, just as she had the week before. She was wearing combat boots and a thin black hoodie with the sleeves rolled up so you could see the tattoos that ran up both of her forearms. After a moment, she nodded and suggested we have a cigarette outside. When I explained my idea about using her in my film, she was quiet for a long time, staring out at the front courtyard, as she mulled it over.

"Would I have to be filmed?"

"Not if you didn't want to be."

"I don't want to be filmed."

"Okay. That's fine. We could maybe just do a voice-over or something. Over some of your artwork."

"I don't want my artwork being filmed either."

"Okay," I said. "So is that a yes?"

"That's a maybe," she said, and then she stood up and turned around and headed back inside the building.

That evening, Carly and I went out to eat with some friends at one of the new taco places in our neighborhood, and on the way home, as we passed by the boarded-up buildings at the far end of our block, I told Carly about my idea to interview Jimena. She shrugged and said, "Does she really qualify as a local artist? I mean, isn't she more of a student?"

"She's local," I said. "And she makes art."

"Have you ever seen it, though? This art that she makes?"

I hadn't, though I don't know why I decided to pretend that I had, why I decided to tell Carly that I'd seen a few pieces that morning and they were good. Carly continued to walk ahead silently, her face expressionless.

"I don't know," I said. "Maybe a bad idea, huh?"

But Carly didn't say anything to this. It was a hot night, and I could tell she wanted to get back to the air-conditioning of our apartment. When we got to the steps of our building, I took her hand, and she squeezed mine back tightly.

2.

There was a studio on the south side of San Antonio that Jimena liked to go to in the mornings to work. It was a communal space, owned by a wealthy patron who rented out the small rooms to struggling artists at a reasonable rate. When Jimena went, it was always at the invitation of one of her friends, who let her work there for free. She also had a studio space at school, but she preferred this space on the south side. It was quieter, she said, more removed. She told me this one morning a few weeks later as we were sitting out on the front steps of the apartment building, sharing a cigarette. We'd been hanging out a little by then, mostly in the late afternoons before Carly got home from work. I'd started by talking to Jimena mainly about her art, doing a kind of preliminary interview for the documentary, but our conversations soon evolved into something else. That day I'd been talking to her about her work habits, her process, and why she didn't keep any of her sculptures in her apartment. She paused for a long time when I mentioned this, then pulled out a cigarette and said she wasn't sure, maybe because none of them was actually finished yet.

"What do you mean?"

"They're not done."

"You've never finished a single sculpture?"

She shrugged but said nothing, and I wondered if the real reason was something else—maybe she didn't want to expose herself, or at least that part of herself, in a place that was so public, a place where she brought so many strangers. A couple of times she'd shown me pictures on her phone—faraway shots of some of the ceramic sculptures she'd made for her classes—*experiments*, she called them, or *assignments* (in other words, not serious work). She showed them to me so quickly, too—flashing them in front of my face for just a brief moment before moving on—that I hardly had a chance to process them. One of them, I remember, was a raven of some sort, or perhaps a blackbird, made out of ceramic; another was a Mexican folk-art mask, cut from wood, depicting a coati. Others were more abstract and, I sensed, more personal to her, the way she scrolled past them so quickly, saying things like *terrible* or *embarrassing*.

In every other way, Jimena seemed so confident, so self-possessed, but when it came to talking about her art, she became suddenly evasive, self-effacing and shy.

That day, as I asked her more about her sculptures, she grew silent and still, staring out at the flowering bougainvillea and the cacti at the far end of the courtyard, her eyes growing soft.

"I think I might be going back to California for a while," she said after a moment, quietly, rubbing her arm.

I looked at her. "I thought you said you had bad memories there."

She drew on her cigarette and stared at me, as if not remembering telling me this or surprised that I knew anything about it.

"I might be gone for a week or so. Maybe longer."

"When?"

"Next month."

"What about your classes?"

She ashed her cigarette and shrugged. "Well, I don't know. I imagine they'll still be here when I get back, right?"

She stood up then and dropped her cigarette onto the steps, ground it out with her foot.

"By the way," she said, "they finally fixed it."

"Huh?"

"My door," she said. "They finally fixed that fucker."

.   .   .

Later that night when Carly got home I could tell that something had happened at work. I could tell by the way she didn't even
say hello or hang up her bag in the hallway, the way she just went
straight into the bedroom and closed the door.

This was how it had been the other time, the time she'd been
laid off, and I felt my body weaken with the thought of this. We were
barely getting by on one income and my savings. Take away Carly's
job, and we'd really be in trouble. When she came out of the room
later that night, though, she said that it wasn't as bad as all that. She
hadn't been fired. It was just that the intern had been promoted.

"Above you?"

"No," she said. "The same level. But it's just as bad."

"Why?"

"Because," she said, "she's twenty-four. I'm twice her age. She's
going to make the exact same amount as me. Maybe more because
she has a master's."

I could see Carly going for the mescal and told her maybe she
shouldn't tonight, reminded her of how bad it had been the last time
she'd gone on a bender, how hungover she'd been the next day.

"It's not going to make things better," I said.

But she ignored me and went for the bottle anyway. "When you
have a job," she said, "a job that makes money, you can say things to
me like that. Until then . . ." But she didn't finish. She just poured the
mescal into her glass and walked out of the room.

Downstairs I could hear Jimena and one of her friends laughing, the steady pulse of techno music in the background. I thought
of what would happen if I just went down there and knocked on her
door. What she'd say to me, what she'd do.

After a while I stood up and walked over to the edge of the
kitchen doorway and looked out across the living room to our bed-

room, where I could see Carly sitting on the edge of the bed in the dark, wearing just her bra and a slip. When she saw me, she raised her glass to her lips, smiled briefly, then turned away.

3.

Looking back, I'm not really sure what it was about Jimena that I enjoyed so much. Maybe it was just the idea that when I was with her I didn't have to think about anything else. She'd show me some weird anime series on Netflix that she was obsessed with or play me some obscure band from Iceland that she was currently listening to or sometimes just show me the stuff that she'd been working on in her sketchbook. Ours was a friendship, nothing more. And though she was beautiful, and though I might have been in love with her, it wasn't a physical attraction, even when she was sitting close to me, her bare leg almost touching mine, as she showed me her sketches or a passage of poetry in some strange literary journal she got. Her apartment was like a teenage artist's fantasy. Posters of punk rock shows from the mid-1980s, Communist propaganda, a World War II gas mask framed in a box, mannequin arms placed strategically on a bookshelf filled with first editions of H. G. Wells and pulp fiction paperbacks. Her kitchen had a giant poster of a Galaxie 500, a picture of Jimena dressed as a very convincing David Bowie circa *Aladdin Sane*, all of these old Mexican photographs and artifacts, signage in Spanish, handwritten notes to herself taped along the walls. And no light at all. There was virtually no natural light in Jimena's apartment ever, which was another reason I loved it so much. It was like descending into some type of futuristic cave where the world outside did not exist.

And so I went there every day—every afternoon while Carly

was at work—and before long we were getting to know each other, we were learning about each other, talking about our lives, sharing war stories from high school, talking about artists and films we both liked. Jimena was always trying to get me to tell her stories about the punk rock scene in San Antonio in the early eighties, about the various bands that would come through here on a regular basis. I could tell she liked hearing these stories in the same way I liked hearing her stories about growing up in Belize and then later Guadalajara and Monterrey. She liked hearing them because they had nothing at all to do with her, because they were about a world and time she didn't know.

Around five or six, I'd usually find an excuse to go upstairs. I'd tell her I had laundry to do or dinner to make. I didn't tell her that it was because I knew Carly would be home soon or because I knew that Carly wouldn't like the looks of what we were doing. In fact, I didn't tell her very much about Carly or about our life upstairs at all.

At the time, Jimena was really into this Venezuelan director Margot Benacerraf, and so we spent a lot of those days talking about her films *Reverón* and *Araya*, and how she hadn't really done very much since then—since the 1950s—when she made them, though apparently, according to Jimena, she was still alive.

"She must be eighty-five, maybe ninety by now," Jimena said one day as we sat in her kitchen drinking wine and looking through a book with stills from *Araya*. "I wonder what she's doing."

Jimena mentioned that *Araya* had premiered at Cannes and ended up sharing the prestigious International Critics Prize with Alain Resnais's *Hiroshima Mon Amour*, though sadly almost no one knew of it now. "Everyone knows Alain Resnais. How many people know Margot Benacerraf?"

I had to admit I'd never heard of her before, and Jimena sighed. She was staring intently at a black-and-white still of two shirtless boys climbing up an enormous white hill that looked like a dune.

"I bet you think that's sand," she said, eyeing the photo, "but it's not."

"No?"

"No," she said. "It's salt."

I looked back at the photo, the white expanse of the hill, the boys' lean bodies cast against it, the sky above cloudless and vast.

Jimena stood up after a moment and walked over to the counter to pour herself another glass of wine. "By the way," she said, as she came back to the table. "I've been talking to your wife."

"What do you mean?"

"We've been having coffee."

"You've been having coffee with my wife?"

"Yes."

"Why?"

"I don't know," she said. "I like her. But also she's been helping me write this grant."

I looked at her, perplexed. Carly hadn't mentioned anything about this to me.

"It's kind of funny, actually. Girlfriend used to ice me. Now she wants to help me out."

I sat up in my chair and steadied my glass.

"Did you mention anything about me coming down here to watch movies?"

"No." She looked at me like I was stupid. "It didn't come up."

Then she looked back at the photo and traced her finger along the curved line of the white dune, mouthing something quietly to herself.

"Araya," she said finally, her eyes growing vacant. "The actual peninsula in Venezuela. Margot Benacerraf said it was like going to the moon."

4.

We used to have a weekly night out, Carly and me. We'd usually go barhopping around the Southtown area of San Antonio, our old neighborhood, or else follow the river up north to the VFW, where they always had music and cheap beer, or even farther north to our favorite bar, Tacoland, where they always had a special of some sort—two-for-one well drinks, half-price margaritas—and always had a crowd that was lively and didn't seem to care that we were a little older than most of the other people there. We liked to drink together because drinking was one of the main things we had in common back then, one of the main things that had brought us together. Lots of couples fight when they drink, but we never did. We always laughed, always looked for ways to make the night last longer. All of those dilapidated icehouses we used to visit in the hot summers, the outdoor bars that were little more than falling-down shacks with ice chests perched in front filled with cold Tecates. Back then we both imagined ourselves artists, both had ideas that we were destined for greatness, and those evenings out we used to talk about our plans, about our future projects, our hopes.

These days, though, the weekly nights out had mostly gone away. Carly preferred to stay inside, to drink at home, and since I didn't drink that much myself anymore—not like I used to—I usually fell asleep before her or else I'd just sit there at the kitchen table and read a magazine as she scrolled through her phone, answering emails from work, her drink at her side. Usually she'd want to talk about the intern and what the intern had done lately, but that night she seemed lost in thought, distracted, so I took the opportunity to ask her about Jimena and what Jimena had told me about their coffees together. I mentioned that I'd run into her earlier that day.

Carly stared at me suspiciously. "You ran into her?"

"Yes," I said. "In the hall."

Carly narrowed her eyes then looked down at her cell phone and typed something, a reply to a text. Finally she sighed and went back to her drink. "It's nothing really. The trustees wanted us to do a kind of outreach program for local artists, particularly young artists, helping them apply for grants and stuff." She sipped her drink and shrugged. "I bumped into her the other day, so I brought it up."

I nodded and leaned back in my chair. "So I take it you don't think she's a drug addict anymore."

"Who knows?" Carly shrugged. "I think she's something."

"What does that mean?"

But she didn't answer. She just went back to her drink, taking a small sip, then stirring the ice cubes with her finger.

"I think something happened to her out in California," she said finally. "Something bad."

"Why do you think that?"

"I don't know," she said, "I just do."

Then she stood up, set her drink down on the table, and walked out of the room.

When Jimena talked about California, she used words like *haunted* or *dead to me*. She said that that was where she'd realized she was an artist, though she did little art there, almost none. What she did do was drink, almost every day, and get high, and take almost every invitation that came her way, including the invitation from the man she almost married, an invitation to come live with him in his apartment in West Hollywood, the biggest apartment she'd ever seen, four bedrooms and a big outdoor deck that overlooked La Cienega Boulevard. That was all she'd say about him though. The rest of the story seemed shrouded in darkness, a kind of darkness that seemed impossible to penetrate. *I was really fucked up*, she'd say whenever I pressed her about it, *and I don't mean on drugs. I mean, in my mind. I was just really, really fucked up.*

I was thinking about this the next morning as I stood at the sink, listening to the sound of Jimena crying downstairs in her apartment. This was shortly after Carly had left for work.

At first I'd thought it might have been one of our other neighbors, or maybe the older woman downstairs who lived next door to Jimena, but then I heard her music go on, something loud and industrial, and I realized it was her. I put down the cup I was washing and stood there listening to the music, this loud industrial rock, thunderous and angry and way too loud for this hour of the morning. I imagined some of our other neighbors would start complaining in a second, pounding on her door and telling her to stop, to shut it off, but for a moment before they did I just stood there and listened to it, imagined her sitting on her couch with her head in her hands, legs crossed, eyes closed, crying or screaming or pounding on something hard.

Later that day, as I was sitting out on our balcony having a cigarette, I saw Jimena walking in the distance. I'm not sure where she was walking, but she was walking quickly and I could see her from almost two blocks away, crossing the street, then walking faster. She was wearing her headphones and a tight black tank top, and she was holding a cigarette in one hand and a paper bag in the other. I wondered what was in the paper bag, where she was headed.

Later, when I was sitting in her apartment having a glass of wine and talking to her about my day, I noticed the paper bag sitting out on her little armoire in the living room, the top of it rolled up tight, the bottom of it soiled in grease.

I thought of asking her what was in there but didn't. It wasn't until later, when she disappeared into the bathroom, that I stood up and walked over to the bag and opened it. I knew I shouldn't be doing this, but I couldn't help myself.

Inside there were all sorts of photographs and postcards, many of them torn and yellowed with age. There were also several letters written in Spanish, a few of which had been folded and refolded so many times I worried they might fall apart in my hands. At the very bottom of the bag there was a locket of dark hair sealed in a Ziploc sandwich bag, a rosary, and a black-and-white photograph of Jimena as a child, or so I assumed, standing on a barren mesa in a nondescript location, staring down at her feet. There was no writing on the back of the photo, no indication of where it was shot.

When Jimena finally returned from the bathroom, this time I did ask her what was in the bag, and without missing a beat she just shrugged and said, "Oh, nothing. Just some *pastelitos*. Want one?"

I shook my head no, though I'd wonder later, sitting in my apartment, what she would have done if I'd said yes.

That evening, Carly had to stay late at work, so I bought my dinner from the taco truck that sat parked across the street from our apartment three out of five nights a week and ate it out on the front steps, as Jimena sat beside me, smoking.

I liked this taco truck, but Jimena refused to patronize it, claiming it wasn't authentic Mexican food. Instead, she opted to walk almost seven blocks in the opposite direction from downtown to a taco truck that she claimed was *más auténtico*.

When I asked her that night how she could tell the difference anyway, she said, "The tortillas. If a taco truck doesn't make its own tortillas, you know it's not the real thing. Watch them across the street. They pull their tortillas out of bags. Store bought. They try to hide it but you can tell."

I stared across the street at the lit interior of the taco truck, where I could see the two guys who worked there leaning over the grill.

"Plus," she added, "no salsa game. You ever had their salsas?"

She laughed lightly to herself and drew on her cigarette then shook her head.

I looked at my watch and tried to calculate how much time I had before Carly got home. Earlier, Jimena had mentioned that they'd been hanging out together a lot lately, almost every day, in the mornings, working on her grant.

"How come I never see you two together then?" I asked.

"Because," she said, "we're top secret."

I looked at her. "Seriously," I said, "where do you hang out?"

"I can't divulge."

I picked up my taco and took a bite, then put it down.

"And you never mention that *we* hang out?"

"Nope."

"Okay."

"You know, she's a nice woman, your wife."

"I know that."

"And you know she wants you to get your shit together."

"I know."

"You gotta be careful there," she said.

"What do you mean?"

But she didn't answer. She just looked over at the far end of the courtyard where she'd set up a little succulent garden earlier in the week. One of the guys who worked at her studio on the south side, an elderly painter named Dennis, collected these plants and had been giving her one or two each day to bring home. By now she had a nice collection of them—dudleya and aloes and agaves—which she'd planted in the ground by the far fence and which Benny had yet to notice or complain about.

That evening she was staring out at an enormous purple echeveria, which she'd brought home the day before in a large ceramic pot. She claimed that this particular echeveria was a very rare type of succulent, at least according to her friend Dennis, that it was very valuable. After a while, she walked out and retrieved the echeveria in its pot and brought it back to the building. She placed this beautiful, strange plant on the steps in front of us and then just sat there, staring at it, her eyes glazing over, her shoulder pressed lightly against mine.

Finally she pulled out her phone and opened up the camera feature.

"I'm going to take a picture and send it to my mother," she said.

"Why?" I said. She almost never mentioned her mother, had said virtually nothing about her in the three weeks I'd known her, only that she was manic-depressive, that she'd been in and out of facilities most of her life, that she was virtually absent from Jimena's life from the age of sixteen on.

"My mother loves plants," she said, looking out to the far end of the front courtyard, then up at the sky where dark clouds were forming, a thunderstorm moving in from the south. "It'll make her happy."

5.

There was also, that spring, the sensation of getting older. It was right there in the mirror, of course, but it was also in other places— the supermarket, where I walked among young people without any of them ever looking up to notice me. It was in the absence of this acknowledgment, I think, that I felt the greatest sadness. It was the reality of being unseen, of walking through life as a ghost.

Around Jimena, however, I always felt seen, and maybe that was a part of it. She was young, or at least younger than me, and she was seeing me, maybe not in a romantic light—not that I was thinking along those lines either—but as a human being, a person walking the earth like her, full of fears and regrets, trying not to mess up.

Though I *was* messing up, and I knew that. I was messing up by spending so much time with her when I should have been spending time by myself, getting my life together, or at least working on my film or some other type of project.

"I don't care *what* you do," Carly said to me once. "But you need to do something. Otherwise, what's the point?"

The point of what? I sometimes wanted to ask, though of course I knew.

What would Carly have said to me any of those afternoons had she caught me sitting in Jimena's apartment, listening to Danzig and smoking pot, or watching one of her obscure Polish documentaries or long-forgotten prize-winning art films from the 1950s? And what was Carly herself doing with Jimena at this time? How did they spend their mornings together when they weren't working on the grant? I sometimes wondered if Carly was drawn to Jimena for the same reasons I was or if it was about something different for her. Maybe something more intimate, more personal. I say this only because of the way Carly would get so evasive, almost defensive, when I'd bring Jimena up, when I'd mention her name. I knew that they were getting closer, that they were forming a friendship, and that this friendship had nothing at all to do with me or with my own friendship with Jimena, but at the same time it seemed strange to me that this could be happening at all, that the two of us, Carly and me, could both be forming unique friendships with the same person, that we could, in a sense, be living both parallel and separate lives.

I thought of bringing this up once with Jimena, but she seemed equally reluctant to talk about Carly or their time together.

"This only works if we don't talk about her," she said to me the one time I'd pressed her about it. We were lying on her couch in the late afternoon, passing a joint back and forth, watching *Araya* for the third or fourth time. Jimena paused the film and put out the joint.

"What's *this?*" I said, sitting up.

"Huh?"

"You just said, *this*. What's *this?*"

She looked at me and laughed. "Fuck if I know," she said. Then she picked up the remote and started the film again. "Just watch the film, okay?"

That evening when I came home, I found Carly sitting out on the balcony beside our kitchen, smoking a cigarette and listening to music on her headphones. This was the way she decompressed these days, sitting out there for at least an hour before she came in. If she didn't do that, she said, she wouldn't be able to do anything productive for the rest of the night.

I knew that something else was going on at work, that the intern who was no longer an intern—who was now some type of development manager, who now met regularly with donors and planned fundraising campaigns—was somehow rising even higher in the ranks, how it was no longer an issue of her simply overshadowing Carly but of her possibly replacing her. Still, Carly never talked about this stuff anymore, never mentioned the intern unless I brought her up directly.

That night, watching her sit out there, I found myself thinking about the older couples on the third floor who used to sit on their balconies almost every night when we first moved in. Back then we were one of the younger couples in the building, both of us still in our early thirties, but now, seven years later, it was us who must have seemed like the old guard. I don't think I could have imagined back then that we'd still be living here in this same apartment all these years later, that we wouldn't have bought a house by now and moved on, that we wouldn't have children, stable jobs.

After a while Carly turned around and smiled at me, mouthed the words *be in soon*, then she turned back to the alley below, her head rocking rhythmically to the music on her iPod, as if in a trance.

When she came in later, I was standing at the stove, working on my famous pozole soup, a recipe Carly herself had taught me. Carly stood there for a moment, watching me, then she put down her bag on the table and went for the bottle of mescal. I could tell that something was bothering her—she seemed more distracted than usual—and after a while, when I pressed her, she admitted she'd had a rough day at work. Among other things, she said, Jimena had bailed on their grant.

"What do you mean?"

"She doesn't want to do it anymore."

"Why not?"

Carly shrugged, and I sensed she felt slighted, maybe even hurt. They'd been getting closer lately, I could tell, though Carly told me very little about their time together.

"I thought you guys were pretty close now."

"Me too," Carly said. "Maybe too close." She looked out toward the balcony. "Anyway, it doesn't look good for me, losing this grant."

"What did they say when you told them she bailed?"

"Nothing, really. A few of them were like, yeah, that girl seemed pretty fucked up."

Carly stood up then and walked over to the fridge to get some more ice. When she sat back down at the table, she looked at me evenly.

"I know it sounds stupid, but I really felt like I was helping her out, you know? It was like the one thing in my life I actually felt kind of good about. Like I was doing something good for someone else."

"You were," I said. "She was lucky to have you."

"Only she didn't care."

"You don't know that."

Carly shrugged. "You know, Evelyn's already submitted three grants on behalf of local artists."

"Who's Evelyn?"

"The intern."

"You've never used her name before."

"I haven't?"

"No," I said. "You haven't."

"Well, it's Evelyn," she said, raising her glass, "and you know what? She's not a fucking intern anymore."

Sometimes it made me sad to see Carly like this, knowing that it wasn't really about this woman in the end, that she was channeling all of this hatred toward her when really it was her own fear of losing her job that was upsetting her.

If it wasn't this intern, I sometimes wanted to say, it would be another.

But I knew she didn't want to hear this anyway.

"It's because I was already fired once," she said to me later that night, as we were sitting on the couch. "Everybody knows it, and so it's like this stain on me. Even though they hired me back, even though they even gave me that little raise last year, it's still a fucking stain."

6.

For a while after that, Jimena disappeared. Or maybe she didn't disappear, but she went into a kind of prolonged avoidance of Carly and me. Maybe what had happened between the three of us had become too intense for her, or maybe it was just the strangeness of it. She once admitted to me that she often felt like a marriage counselor who was seeing both of us separately or other times like a mistress, though one who didn't actually *do* anything with either of us.

"A platonic mistress," she said. "There should be a name for that."

"How about just a friend," I said. "Why make it complicated?"

"Because it *is* complicated," she said. "Haven't you noticed?"

We were sitting out on the stoop the evening she said this. Our usual routine. The neighborhood was quiet. A few kids out riding their bikes, a few of the other tenants in the building making short ribs in a smoker in the middle of the front courtyard. The sun was setting in the distance, and I could see the tall buildings downtown.

"I think I need to take a break from you guys," she said after a while, sipping on her drink.

"Why?" I said.

"I don't know," she said. "I just do."

Then she stood up, put her cup down on the steps, and headed back inside.

That night I stood in the hallway on the second floor and listened to Jimena and Carly talking downstairs. I couldn't make out what they were saying to each other, but I could hear the rise and fall of their voices, the conversation growing more and more intense as time passed. Later Carly would return and explain to me that Jimena was leaving for California the next week, that this was what they'd been talking about, but at the moment it seemed to me to be about more than just that.

"Did she say what day she was leaving?" We were standing in the kitchen, smoking.

"No." Carly shook her head. "She just said next week." Then she looked down at her phone as if looking for a specific message, studied it briefly, then walked out of the room.

Carly didn't want to do much that night. We had a quiet dinner together then went to bed early, but at some point later I woke to the sound of a dog barking outside and noticed Carly sitting out on the side balcony by herself, her body silvered in moonlight. She had her headphones on and was rocking back and forth slowly, hugging herself. I stood at the window and watched her for a while. I couldn't see her face, but from the back, the way she was hunched over, her shoulders pinched, it almost seemed for a moment like she was crying.

7.

Over the next couple of weeks not much happened, though Jimena's aunt from the north side stopped by twice. I recognized her aunt from the photos that Jimena had shown me of her in her apartment—an older lady with a strong, dignified presence about her, long, dark hair, high cheekbones, pretty. The first time she stopped by I was sitting out on the front steps, smoking a cigarette, and I let her pass without saying a word.

When she came back again, though, the next week, I felt obligated to stop her. I was on the steps again, drinking my coffee.

"You looking for Jimena?" I said.

She looked at me, perplexed, then guarded, as if she didn't know how I'd know this.

"You've seen her?"

"She's out in California," I said, "or at least that's where she said she was going."

She nodded, and then her face darkened, as if I'd confirmed some deep fear of hers. "*Polilla a una llama,*" she said finally.

"What's that?"

"Just an expression," she said. "In Spanish it means 'moth to a flame.'"

I nodded.

The truth was, the longer Jimena had been in California, the more I'd begun to wonder what it had meant to her, what had happened out there. Once or twice she'd alluded to a group of artist friends and of course there was the man she almost married, though she never said anything more about him, not even his name. Sometimes I imagined a wealthy movie producer drawn in by Jimena's beauty; other times it was a bad boy, a bassist in a punk band, a drug dealer, a troubled actor. In all likelihood, though, this man, whoever he was, was much more tepid than all that.

I was almost married, she'd said to me more than once, as if this were a tragedy narrowly avoided.

I thought of bringing this up to her aunt that day she stopped by, but instead I just smiled and gave her my number and told her she could call me anytime if she wanted me to go down and check if Jimena was there. "Easier than you driving all the way down here," I said.

"Right." She nodded, and then she reached out slowly and took my hand, stared at me plaintively. "Thank you," she said softly. "I will be back."

. . .

As it turned out, Jimena was gone only a couple of weeks, not long enough for her to lose her job or her enrollment status at the Southwest School of Art. When she returned, her hair was shorter and she had a new tattoo on the nape of her neck, a small Spanish word, *olvidados*, written in black cursive. I passed her coming up the steps from the laundry room in the basement, carrying a basket of damp black jeans and T-shirts.

"Dryer's broken," she said and shrugged. "Fucking Benny."

I asked her if she needed any help and she said no. "So how was California?" I added, as she started down the hall toward her apartment.

"Don't ask," she said over her shoulder without looking back.

"That bad?"

She nodded, again without looking back, then stopped at her door and put her basket on the ground. I watched her without saying anything as she fumbled for her keys.

"Still," she said, "I'm probably going to go back there for a while."

"What do you mean?"

She continued to fumble with her keys.

"To visit?"

"No." She shook her head, still looking down. Finally she found her key and slid it in the lock. Then she looked at me. I could feel my heart racing.

"What about your classes?"

She shrugged. "They have art schools in California, believe it or not."

I looked at her. "I mean, what about the work you've been doing?"

"That work's not going anywhere."

I stood there, motionless, trying to get a read on her face. "Is this about that guy you almost married?"

She looked down but didn't say anything.

"It's about a lot of things," she said finally and then turned and headed back inside her apartment.

Carly had a benefit she was organizing that afternoon at one of the smaller galleries on the south side, and I had promised to make us both dinner and clean the apartment before she returned, but at that moment all I could think about was Jimena leaving, not being here anymore, and what that would mean to us. I stood in the hall, studying my hands, trying to orient myself.

After a while, Jimena's door opened again and she stuck her head out and stared at me intently. Our eyes met for just a brief moment and then she smiled, turned around slowly, and said, "You want to watch a movie?"

8.

Another thing about *Araya*: it's a documentary but it doesn't feel like a documentary. It feels like a work of fiction. It has that same type of poetic feel, that mood. There are characters in it, characters played by local salt miners, and it has an experimental form and structure. After Benacerraf finished it, she went on to head a number of Venezuelan film and cultural organizations, but she never made another film. When I asked Jimena if Benacerraf ever returned to the island where she'd made her masterpiece, she said, yes, many years later she went back.

"But almost all of the people who had lived and worked there were gone by then. What was left was just a ghost town."

I nodded.

"But I don't like to think about that anyway," she said. "I just like to remember it the way it was in the film."

"Why?"

"Because," she said, "at the end of the film there's still hope, you know? You don't know what's going to happen to these people yet. It's still possible they might find better lives."

"But they don't," I said.

"I know," she said. "But at the end of the film, you know, nobody knows that yet."

9.

When Jimena's aunt called us three months later to ask if we had any idea where Jimena was—if we'd seen her or heard from her—I had to tell her the truth, which was that we hadn't heard from or seen her since the week she left. All I knew was that she'd gone back to L.A., but her aunt already knew this. "She's doing it again," she said. "It's not the first time." She then said something vague about the man out there, who she first referred to as a *pendejo* and later as a *sucio*.

"He's probably going to kill her," she said.

"What do you mean?" I said.

But she wouldn't explain.

"The last time I saw her was actually about a week or so before she left," I said. "She didn't really say goodbye to us."

"Typical," she said, "right?"

I said nothing.

"Is that why she went back there?" I said finally. "For him?"

"No. Not for him," she said. "For her daughter."

"She has a daughter?"

"Oh *hijo*," she said. "You really don't know anything about her, do you?"

I was silent.

"And I bet you fell in love with her, too, didn't you?"

I thought then of a conversation I'd had with Jimena a few days before she left and how I'd asked her if anything physical had ever happened between her and Carly. Jimena just rolled her eyes and laughed. "So typical," she'd said. "Why do guys always think it's about sex?" Then she'd walked away, still shaking her head.

Her aunt was now silent on the other end of the line, still waiting for my response.

"You did," she said finally, "didn't you?"

"No," I said and looked out the window at the palm trees in the distance. "It was never about that."

In the days and weeks that followed, Carly and I moved through our apartment like ghosts, trying to figure out a way to be together again, a way to move forward from whatever it was that had happened to our lives those past few months.

Later we would call it a random interlude. We'd give it names, like that really fucked-up period when Jimena was living downstairs, or those strange days when you-know-who was always around. But for a while we missed her, missed her in the way one misses a parent during those first few weeks of college. We missed the comfort of knowing she was around, of knowing there was someone else there besides just us.

And for a while after that, Carly went into a kind of quiet phase herself. She spent a lot of time out on the side balcony on her own, listening to music, smoking. Sometimes she'd talk about the possibility of having a child again, something she hadn't talked about in a while. She was thirty-nine, she'd say, it would be difficult, yes, and there would be risk, but it was still possible. After a while, though, this talk seemed to disappear, sucked up by the pressures at her work, the growing uncertainty about her future.

As for me, I eventually got a job, a part-time job doing sound production for the film institute in town. It wasn't a high-paying job, but it got me out of the house four or five mornings a week. I'd given up on the documentary by then.

Still, I remember one night a few months after Jimena's aunt called us about Jimena's disappearance. I was sitting on the balcony with Carly and playing some of the audio of Jimena talking about her art. She still hadn't resurfaced yet—in fact, she never would—and it was strange hearing her voice on the recording. The audio was garbled and staticky but it was still distinctly her: *I think it's pointless to hope for others to connect with your artwork*, she was saying. *Anytime I'm making anything I'm thinking about my immediate community. . . . The artists I respect don't intellectualize their art or even try to talk about it. Does that make sense?* she said quietly. *Do you know what I mean?*

After that, I turned off the recording, and Carly leaned her head on my shoulder. We looked out at the buildings in the distance, the soft glimmering lights of downtown San Antonio. It was a cold night, one of the coldest nights in recent memory, the air so brisk you could see your breath. Downstairs in the courtyard, I could hear people talking, a party starting up, someone playing guitar. I pulled Carly in closer, wrapped my arms around her, took her hand in mine.

"You know," I said after a moment, lacing my fingers through hers, looking out at the buildings, "sometimes I wonder where we went, Car."

"What do you mean?"

"I don't know."

"We didn't *go* anywhere," she said. "And sometimes I wonder if that's the problem."

I looked at her. "But you know what I mean," I said. "Sometimes I find myself trying so hard to hold on to that idea of who I used to be, you know? It's so painful to let that go."

She nodded. "But you're not that different, really," she said. "Neither of us are."

"I'm definitely not any more accomplished," I said. "Or wiser."

"No," she said, "but it's not about that anyway. None of that stuff really matters." She squeezed my hand and picked up her drink and took a long sip, then stared at me again. "Do you really think you're that different from the person you used to be?"

"I don't know," I said. "I'm more patient maybe. I definitely expect less of myself."

"Do you think you're any easier on yourself?"

"No," I said. "I just expect less."

She smiled and leaned her head on my shoulder. At that moment it wasn't hard to see how either of us might have been drawn in by Jimena, how anyone like us might have been.

As for Jimena, I wasn't really sure what she got out of it. Our time together. Those long, lazy days in her apartment. Maybe it was just having someone there to distract her, another body in her living room. I'd been together with Carly so long I sometimes forgot how comforting that could be when you're single, just having someone else in your space, another body there, another human being to talk to.

The Empty Unit

Our landlord, Manuel, kept one of the apartments on our hallway empty, the one at the far end overlooking the courtyard below. During those first few months that we lived there, my wife, Stephanie, and I would often hear him letting himself into the unit at night, playing his Tito Puente and Ella Fitzgerald records, the sound of Santitos Colón's vocals echoing down the hall. There was a woman who lived right next door to us, an older woman named Estelle, and she'd occasionally complain about it, but for the most part nobody said a word. Manuel was our landlord after all. It was his building. He could do what he wanted. But still, there was something haunting about it, the way he'd show up sometimes very late at night and disappear inside that unit, playing his records and doing who knows what. Sometimes we'd smell cigarette smoke wafting from under the door, and I sometimes imagined him drinking in there, though I never had evidence of that. From what I'd gathered the apartment was mostly unfurnished. Estelle had told us there was a couch in there and a little table and a refrigerator but that was about it. Estelle also speculated that Manuel was going through a divorce and was keeping the unit empty as a kind of backup plan should he ever actually need it to live. *He's mourning his wife,* Estelle would say, on those evenings she'd invite us over for tea or coffee with cinnamon. *He's mourning the end of his marriage.* This went on for a couple of months or more, through most of that quiet summer. Then suddenly it stopped. Manuel stopped appearing at night and the sounds of Tito Puente's orchestra disappeared as well.

She's taken him back, Estelle informed us one evening, as we were coming out of our unit. *I'm almost sure of it.*

The Disappeared

I have a photograph of Daniel on the last day I ever saw him. This would have been in 2005, just after we'd moved into our first house in San Antonio, our starter house, as my wife still refers to it now. In the picture, Daniel is standing next to me on our back deck, his arm draped loosely around my shoulder, his eyes glazed from all the wine we'd consumed earlier that day. It's early evening in the picture, and summertime. You can see the flowering bougainvillea that's cascading over the top of our back fence, and all of the little cacti that Tanya, my wife, had collected that year for her succulent garden. When I look at that picture now, I think as much about our old lives in that house as I do about Daniel. But of course the one obvious difference is that that house is still there, whereas Daniel isn't.

. . .

When I first learned of Daniel's disappearance, it was from his girlfriend at the time, Antoinette, who called me up one night shortly after Daniel had gone missing on the Fortynine Palms Oasis Trail in Joshua Tree National Park. I hadn't seen Daniel in quite some time, maybe seven months, which was unusual given our closeness. He was living in Austin at the time, and I knew that he'd been traveling a lot more in the past year or so, taking several trips up to Yellowstone and also to Alaska. I hadn't known about his latest trip to Joshua Tree, though I knew he'd made several trips out there in the past. According to Antoinette, he'd actually gone out to Joshua Tree three times in the past six months, once with her and the other two times alone, and was even thinking about buying a second home out there, near Riverside. Antoinette explained all of this to me the night she called, a few weeks after the start of the fall semester, a balmy evening in late September when I was running a group critique for one of my advanced evening drawing classes.

As I stood out on the balcony beside the studio where I teach, my worried students staring out at me through the glass window, Antoinette went over everything she knew: how Daniel had been missing for almost forty-eight hours, how the last contact she'd had with him directly was the morning of his last solo excursion, a phone call he'd made to her from his motel room in Yucca Valley, and how the search and rescue mission had so far turned up nothing, not even a footprint or a water bottle or an item of clothing from the trail he'd been hiking on. All they'd found was his Subaru, untouched, parked in the Cottonwood Visitor Center near the trailhead to the Fortynine Palms Oasis Trail, his cell phone locked in the glove box. She then explained that the main reason she'd called me was because she knew I was one of Daniel's closest friends, that he talked about me all the time, and that she thought I'd want to know. She also said that a group of his Austin friends as well as his family from Houston were getting together that weekend to share information and have a kind of prayer vigil. If I wanted to join them, she said, I was welcome.

The whole conversation was a lot to process, and I don't remember very much else from that night, only that I went into the classroom and said something brief to my students about an unexpected emergency and then I drove toward my house, only I didn't go there. Instead I went to a bar that Daniel and I used to go to back in college, whenever we were home on break, a Mexican place that served these two-dollar Tecates and Coronas and Buds. I sidled up next to a bunch of the older patrons at the bar and proceeded to get drunk by myself. Daniel was thirty-three years old at the time. He was a baby by most people's standards. He still had all of his hair, still had a runner's body, still looked effortlessly fit. He had made all of this money working for Dell the past few years, so much money that I'd often found myself shamefully envious of it, even bitter about it, all of his sudden wealth—his new house out in the Westlake Hills, his swimming pool, his personal trainer. But now all I could think about was how sad it was, how tragic it was, really, that he might never have a chance to spend even half of the money he'd made. I knew that Antoinette had wanted to make it sound better than it was, more hopeful, but I could tell that it was dire. It was dire or she'd never be calling me like this, in such a panic.

I'd told her that I still had a couple of classes I had to teach that week—classes I couldn't really get out of—but that I'd be up over the weekend to help out and attend the vigil if he still hadn't turned up. Then I'd hung up and went in to see my students and then off to the bar. But I never did make it up to Austin that weekend—I had a sudden commitment at school, an emergency involving a colleague of mine and a student—and by the time I did make it up there, the following week, there wasn't much hope left and almost everyone who had been there before was gone, everyone except for Antoinette and Daniel's family.

I don't have many regrets in my life but I do regret never making it out to Daniel's house that weekend. From everything I've since learned, it wouldn't have made much difference—it was just a few of his friends, his family, and Antoinette, everyone coming together to share information and comfort each other, but still, I would have liked to have been there to be a part of it.

By then, of course, the search and rescue had been called off, and by then, of course, there wasn't much hope, but Antoinette hadn't told me any of that during our phone conversation (or in any of her subsequent emails). Months later, when I was helping her organize Daniel's belongings, I told her that I wished she'd leveled with me sooner and that I wished she'd called me earlier. She paused then—we were standing out by the pool in Daniel's backyard a few days after the funeral; I'd driven up that morning from San Antonio to help her out with the packing up of the house, a task that seemed like it might take several days—and she was standing now with her back to the pool. She said that he'd actually been missing for almost four days at the time she called me.

"Four days?" I said.

"Yes," she said. "But please don't hate me."

I looked over at the flowering plumbago at the far end of Daniel's yard, the palm trees and the sagebrush. I thought of all the stupid stuff I'd been doing during that time Daniel was missing.

"You had a lot on your plate," I said finally to Antoinette, touching her arm. "There's no way of knowing the right thing to do in these situations."

"His parents told me they wanted to keep it quiet."

"I'm sure," I said. "And you were trying to respect their wishes."

"I was," she said. "I felt I had to."

"And you did."

Antoinette looked away then. I was trying to be supportive, understanding, but a part of me still resented her for not telling me sooner, and I could tell that she could sense this. Antoinette was from France originally and she'd been living in the States for almost three years, but I had no idea whether she'd been living here legally or not. I knew that she didn't work, and I knew that she wasn't in school for anything. From what I could tell she had met Daniel at a party a few years back and had been living with him ever since. Daniel rarely talked about her when we met up, which made me think they weren't that serious, and when I'd asked him once if they were going to get married, he'd just laughed and said maybe, maybe not. Then he'd laughed again. "Antoinette," he said. "She's a piece of work, my friend. I love her to death, but she's a piece of work." That's all he'd said, and again I'd taken this to mean they weren't that close, but now it looked like Antoinette had basically assumed the role of his common-law wife. I would have assumed that she was in this partly for his money, that she hoped to be included in his will, or in the settlement of his estate, but according to her, Daniel had left almost everything in his will to his family—to his brothers and sisters, his parents. She didn't seem bitter about this or disappointed at all, which made me think that she might have genuinely loved him.

"And you weren't upset that he never included you?" I asked her. This was later that day, after we'd finished most of the living room and pantry. We were standing in Daniel's kitchen now, sunlight filling the room, though it was nearly six.

"I told him I didn't want to be included. If I was his wife, that would be one thing, but I wasn't his wife."

"And what did he say?"

"He tried to insist, but in the end he respected my wishes."

I looked at her. She was putting bottles of wine into boxes and wrapping them with tape. It was early evening, and I could see the sun setting outside the window beside the pool.

"Besides," she said. "I want to stay close to his family—it's important to me—and I don't want them ever questioning my motives for being with him."

"Have they been up here a lot," I said, "to help?"

"Only that one time," she said. "Isn't that bizarre? You've come here more than them."

"Maybe they're still in denial."

She shrugged. "If it wasn't for me, the house would just be sitting here, filled with his things."

"And you've been staying here still?" It was an obvious question perhaps, but I realized then that I'd never asked it officially, that I had no idea whether she had moved out or not.

"Yes," she said. "And it doesn't make me sad, actually. I thought it would, but it doesn't. If anything, it makes me feel closer to him. Sometimes I still sleep with his clothes."

I looked out the window then and noticed a flock of birds, grackles maybe, flying over the backyard. The pool had started to collect leaves, and the grass hadn't been cut in several weeks. Antoinette had explained to me earlier that she'd let the maintenance guys go, as she didn't have the money to pay them anymore and didn't feel comfortable asking Daniel's family.

"Do you know where you'll go next?" I said.

She looked up from the box she was taping. Then she stood up and grabbed one of the loose bottles on the counter and looked at it, then smiled. "Do you want to drink this?" she said, showing me the bottle. "It isn't cheap."

I pretended to study the label, though I knew almost nothing about wine. "I still have to find a place to stay tonight," I said. "If we're going to pack up the rest of this stuff tomorrow, I'll need my rest."

"You could stay here," she said. "Out in the cabana house, or even on the couch if you'd like."

I thought about this, and then I thought about Tanya back in San Antonio and what I'd tell her. Antoinette was a beautiful woman, and I knew what Tanya might think, even if it was the last thing on my own mind. I'd told Tanya earlier that I was coming up here for a couple of days to help Antoinette out, to help her as a kind of gesture of good-will. I knew that it was something that Daniel would have wanted me to do, I said. She'd balked at the idea at first, but had finally relented. Staying over at the house, though, wasn't part of the deal.

"Let me think about it," I said, but Antoinette was already getting out glasses by then, already pouring the wine.

"Are you hungry?" she said. "I could make us something to eat, too."

In the last email I'd received from Daniel he'd written a lot about wanting to return to France, where he'd lived for a year after college, backpacking around with a bunch of our mutual friends, and how he still thought about that year as the happiest in his life. He also added that he thought that part of his attraction to Antoinette had to do with that, with the fact that she reminded him of that year and of that time in his life. She was very traditionally French, he'd written, though he didn't explain what he meant by this. He also wrote that she reminded him of a girl he'd dated over there named Claire, but unlike Claire, he wrote, Antoinette was very kind, very loving. This was the closest he'd ever come to actually describing how he felt about Antoinette, but from what I could gather, or from what I had managed to piece together, it was complicated.

Tanya thought it was strange that he'd never invited us up there to meet her, that he'd kept their relationship a secret, but I never saw it that way. I knew that Daniel was a private person and that he tended to be protective of his relationships, especially if they were serious. I'd actually met Antoinette twice before, both times when she and Daniel were passing through town on their way out to Marfa, and this was the reason I had her number in my phone. On both occasions, Daniel had asked me to meet them privately. He loved Tanya, of course, but I think he sensed intuitively that she wouldn't approve of Antoinette if they met, and I think he was probably right. Tanya had always been protective of Daniel. She looked over him in a sisterly way, especially since he'd started making money, and she'd always been suspicious of his girlfriends. She'd taken the news of his disappearance hard, probably as hard as me, and had been inconsolable for several weeks afterward, too sad to even come up for the funeral. I'd actually asked her to come up with me that weekend—to help out with the house—but she said she couldn't. She said that she didn't think she could ever step inside that house again.

It was strange, but things had been tense between us the past few months, and I couldn't say why. If anything, I would have thought that Daniel's disappearance would have brought us closer together but it hadn't. Tanya had taken off a few weeks from work—she had over a month's worth of vacation time saved up and had figured this was as good a reason as any to use it—but I hadn't actually seen her that much over the past month. She'd taken to running and working out in the mornings, and spent her evenings lying on the couch, binge-watching shows that I'd never heard of, or staring at her computer screen, trying to compose emails to people I didn't know. On the few occasions when I'd suggested we do something—go out to dinner or maybe grab a drink—she'd said that she wasn't really in the right state of mind to be in public right now. I'd asked her what she meant by this, but she hadn't elaborated. I think on some level the two of us just handled grief differently. When something traumatic happened, my natural instinct was to talk about it, to get it all off my chest, whereas Tanya was much more introverted and reclusive. Her natural instinct was to put up a wall around herself, to cocoon herself inside a blanket on the couch and not talk to anyone. Still, we'd been distant with each other even before Daniel's disappearance, and now I was worried that things were getting worse.

I'd asked her to come up with me that morning—had begged her really—but she'd adamantly refused. She claimed that it would simply be too painful for her, but I knew that it was more than that. I knew that she didn't want to spend an hour and a half alone with me in the car. I knew that she didn't want to have to meet Antoinette and talk to her. And I knew that she didn't want to be around all of Daniel's stuff and be reminded of what had happened.

"I'll call you as soon as I get there," I said to her as I stood in the doorway that morning. She was lying on the couch at the time, a blanket wrapped around her body. She'd spent the night there.

"I might be on a run," she said.

"I'll leave a message."

"Call me tonight," she said. "Before you go to sleep, okay?"

"Okay," I said.

But I hadn't called her before I went to sleep. Antoinette and I had finished off the bottle of wine she'd opened and then we'd opened another. We might have had two or three bottles after that, I'm not sure, and then I went down to Daniel's liquor cabinet in the basement and brought up several more bottles, all whiskeys. Antoinette had passed out by then on the living room couch, and so I sat down at the island in the middle of the kitchen and turned down the lights and proceeded to get drunk by myself. It had been a long time since I'd been on a bender like this, maybe five or six years, and I realized that my body had needed it. I ended up passing out on one of the chaise lounge chairs by the pool, and I must have tried to go into the water at one point, I think, because I was stripped down to my boxer shorts and holding a half-inflated raft when Antoinette discovered me the next morning around eight.

She was standing in a T-shirt and sweatpants, holding a package of frozen peas to her head.

"Do you want a glass of water?" she said. "Aspirin?"

"I'm actually okay," I said, and I was. Surprisingly, I was not hungover at all.

"I'm going to go back to sleep for a little while, okay? Make yourself anything you want from the fridge. And wake me up if I sleep too long."

She turned around then and went back to the house, and I lay there for a while longer, staring up at the morning sky, which was bright and cloudless, thinking about Tanya and whether or not I should call her.

After a while, I went back inside and made myself some oatmeal with fruit, some wheat toast, a glass of orange juice. I thought about what had happened the night before, but most of it was murky. I remembered talking to Antoinette about Daniel, and then about her childhood in Lower Normandy in the northern part of France. I remembered her telling a story about her grandfather—or maybe it was an uncle—building a somewhat primitive piano from scratch, and another relative, maybe an aunt, working for the Royal Opera House in London as an archivist. She had a lot of strange stories, and the longer she talked the stranger they got. At one point she went into the living room and never came out. When I went in to check on her she was passed out, so I went down to the basement by myself in search of the booze.

Later that night, after I'd found myself a comfortable spot on the back deck, by the pool, I heard what I thought was Antoinette crying, wailing almost, like an animal. I remembered sitting there, wondering if I should turn around and go back in, check on her, but then I thought it might be embarrassing for both us, so I didn't. Instead, I leaned back in the chair and closed my eyes. I closed my eyes and I listened.

Now I wondered if I'd done the right thing by not going in. Maybe she'd expected me to come in and comfort her, maybe she'd wondered where I was. I looked around the kitchen at the mess we'd made and then walked into the living room, where I found most of the packing supplies she'd bought: the bubble wrap and heavy-duty packaging tape, the newspapers and boxes, the scissors and labels, everything she thought we might need. I sat down on the couch and started to assemble one of the cardboard boxes from the pack on the floor. Upstairs, I knew that she was sleeping and probably would be for some time, so I started picking up various things—picture frames and ashtrays and table lamps—and wrapping them up in newspaper and then placing them in the box. After I finished one box, I moved on to another, and then another after that. Pretty soon I had half the room packed up. In the smaller boxes I'd placed all of the books and heavier items, in the larger boxes all of the fragile stuff. I realized that I was sweating now, that I was feeling a little light-headed.

By noon, when Antoinette finally came down, I had packed up almost the entire living room and most of Daniel's study. I had lined up all of the boxes in the hallway and labeled the ones I could. Antoinette stared at everything I'd done and then smiled.

"I should have slept longer." She laughed.

I was soaked in sweat by then, my shirt drenched. The only things I hadn't packed up were the original pieces of art that Daniel had hung on his walls. Some of these pieces were very expensive, I knew, and others were deeply personal. I didn't know if Antoinette had any plans for them. A few of the pieces were actually lithographs I had done in grad school and given to him, and one of the linocuts in his study was a print I'd made in college. It was a bit embarrassing to look at all of this old work, all of my juvenilia, as my wife, Tanya, would put it. It was tantamount to looking at an old photograph of yourself from high school and thinking, did I really used to wear my hair that way?

Still, it had always touched me that Daniel had chosen to display my work around his house, even if it was early work, embarrassing work. As Antoinette explained to me later that day, as we were working on the family room, it was one of the ways he stayed close to me. "That's how he always explained it to me," she said. "He'd look at one of your prints, and he'd feel that you were there. Even if you weren't. Even if you were very far away."

We were sitting on the floor in the family room, packing up DVDs into boxes, and seeing all of the titles—*Le Circle Rouge, Delicatessen, Cléo from 5 to 7*—felt a little like going back in time, like we were back in our old apartment on Seventh Street or the one we lived in later in Barton Springs. This was all before Austin changed, of course, back when it was still just a sleepy college town. People my age like to wax nostalgic about those days, the early nineties in Austin, like we're talking about Paris in the twenties, or Berkeley in the sixties, but it really felt that way sometimes, and I think we were all very aware of the fact that we were living in a very special place at a very special time in that place's history and that it probably wouldn't last. And of course, it didn't last. The Austin of today barely resembles the Austin of our youth, or of our college and grad school years, at least, but I try not to think about that now when I visit. I try not to think about what Daniel used to call "The Last Days of April," a reference to some poem he'd once read, a poem by a poet whose name I no longer recall.

"I think it's almost cocktail hour," Antoinette was saying now. This was later that day, after we'd finished the family room—or at least most of it—and were now back in the kitchen, looking for something to eat. Antoinette had found a loaf of sourdough bread and some fresh tomatoes and I'd found about a half pound of Gruyère and some olive oil and garlic. Together we were able to piece together something resembling an open-faced bruschetta-slash-grilled cheese sandwich. We assembled what we had on a cookie sheet and slid it into the oven to broil.

"It might not look pretty," she said. "But I bet it'll taste good." Then she turned around and went downstairs to find more wine.

When she came back up, a few minutes later, she was holding several bottles of red and my cell phone.

"You must have left it down there last night," she said, handing me the phone. "It was beeping."

And I realized then that I'd gone the entire day without looking at it. When I unlocked the screen, I saw that there were seven missed calls and four new messages, all from Tanya.

I told Antoinette I'd be back in a minute and then took the phone out to the backyard by the pool. It was hot out, easily a hundred degrees, and I immediately started sweating. I sat down on the cement deck next to the pool and dangled my feet in the water, but the water wasn't even cold now. It was tepid, like bathwater.

When Tanya finally picked up, she sounded drowsy. Not angry, though. Just tired.

"I've been calling all day," she said.

"I know," I said. "I'm sorry." I could tell that something was wrong. "What's going on?"

"I don't know," she said. "I think it's just the fact there was actually a funeral, you know?" She paused. "It's like it's actually final now."

I said nothing.

"I just can't stop thinking about him, I guess. It's like my brain's stuck in a loop, and I can't shut it off."

"Have you tried reading?" I said. "Watching TV?"

"You know how much stuff on TV is about death? You don't realize it until someone you know dies, and then it's like everywhere. You can't find a single show that doesn't remind you of the very thing you're trying to forget."

I didn't know what to say to her. "I miss you," I said finally.

"I miss you, too," she said, and was quiet. "Maybe I just wanted to hear your voice."

When I went back inside, I found Antoinette sitting at the island in the middle of the kitchen, blowing on one of our sandwich creations.

"They're still hot," she said, nodding to the other ones on the cookie sheet. "But they smell good."

I sat down on the other side of the island and reached for the wine she'd opened.

"I didn't know if you wanted red or white," she said.

"Red's fine," I said, pouring myself a glass.

"This feels like a familiar scene," she said, "doesn't it?"

"How so?"

"I don't know." She shrugged. "It just does."

I looked at her. "Did you guys used to cook a lot?"

"Yes," she said. "All the time. Daniel was a terrible cook, of course, but he enjoyed it so much I never had the heart to tell him." She laughed. Then she looked out the window, where the sun was now setting, and I asked her to tell me about Daniel's last few months, those last few months of his life when I hadn't seen him.

"They were actually pretty peaceful," she said, putting down her glass. "Kind of calm, actually. He traveled by himself out to Joshua Tree a few times, Big Bend, and when he came back he was always very relaxed about everything, you know, even work, which he usually never was." She looked at me. "And that's around the time he had the idea about buying another place out there, in Riverside. He was really getting into it, you know? Being out there for long stretches by himself."

I nodded.

Antoinette picked up her glass and took a sip. "It's strange, but sometimes I find myself still thinking it might be some type of joke, you know, like a trick he's been playing on us. You know how he was always designing those elaborate tricks?"

"Yeah," I said, "only what would be the point?"

"That's the problem," she said. "There isn't one."

She put down her glass and ran her finger along the counter. "And sometimes, you know—and I know this is crazy—but sometimes I still think he might show up or that someone might find him, you know?"

I nodded. "Me too," I said.

"The human heart resists it, I think, on some level. The idea of someone just disappearing like that. It's not a thing we can fully comprehend."

I picked up the bruschetta and took a small bite. "Have you ever thought he might have wanted to do it intentionally?"

"Disappear?"

"Or end things."

"Sure," she said. "Of course. I've thought about it a lot. He was unhappy, you know. At work, especially. He talked about it sometimes. But he was never unhappy when he was out there." She picked up her wineglass and took a sip, glanced out the window at the garden. "And then you talk to the police and they think it might have been foul play, but who in the world would have wanted to hurt him? He barely knew anybody, you know? He barely had any friends." She looked at me. "It seems impossible."

I nodded. "I've never thought that's what it was."

"Me neither," she said. "Although the world is full of fucked-up people, right?"

"That's true," I said. "It definitely is."

She looked at me then sipped her wine. "And if that's what he chose, you know—the *other*—if he chose silence, then that's fine. It's his silence, and it's a mystery and it's not for us to understand. But I can tell you he was never unhappy when he was out there, in Joshua Tree." She stared at me. "Never."

We worked through the rest of the night, bringing the wine with us, as we moved from room to room, first finishing up the downstairs and the garage, and then moving upstairs to the guest room and the master bedroom. There was a sadness in the air as you got closer to the master bedroom, or at least it seemed that way to me, and I could tell that Antoinette was strangely protective of it, that she didn't want me to see how she'd been keeping it up.

"I'll do that room myself," she said, as she saw me moving toward it with the vacuum.

"Okay," I said. It must have been four in the morning by then, almost dawn, and we were both exhausted, our T-shirts clinging to our backs, our hands and forearms covered with scrapes. I sat down in the hallway outside the master bedroom and leaned against the wall, and Antoinette sat down beside me.

"There's really not much left for you to help with," she said. "I can do the rest myself tomorrow or Monday."

"And Daniel's parents are coming up Tuesday?"

She nodded. "But they don't even know what he has here, and I doubt they have anywhere to put it." She looked at me. "You know, you should take something. A photograph, a painting. They'll never miss it."

I nodded, and thought about what I'd take if I could. Daniel's parents had lived in San Antonio when we were in college—he'd grown up there, like me—but now they lived in Houston. Before the funeral, I hadn't seen them in probably seven or eight years, and they'd barely acknowledged me at the service. Still, I'd been strangely touched by his father's speech. He'd always struck me as a hard-ass, a military type, but he spoke so eloquently about his son's childhood, about that time when I hadn't known him, and how sensitive Daniel had been back then. He finished by saying in a quiet, almost inaudible voice that nothing in his life had prepared him for the incomprehensible task of burying his own child. He looked down as he said this, his hands shaking, and something in my body shifted.

Antoinette was standing up now and walking toward the packing supplies at the end of the hall.

"I think I'm going to take a swim," she said. "I can't seem to cool down. Do you want to join me?"

She was already walking down the staircase as she said this, though, already disappearing from sight.

.   .   .

The pool that Daniel had installed several years ago when he purchased the house was an infinity style pool, one of those shapeless, modern designs that seems to have a vanishing edge, an edge that merges with the horizon, or the sky, and seems to create the effect of water without boundary. I'd only swum in this pool once or twice before, despite visiting his house many times, maybe because Daniel himself rarely used it. He was much more interested in hanging out *by* the pool, it always seemed, than actually getting in. As Tanya once put it, he seemed to have bought a pool for purely aesthetic reasons.

Still, it was a beautiful piece of craftsmanship—he'd hired an architect to design it—and after a day of sweating in the summer heat, of boxing up fragments of my friend's life like they were pieces of a discarded puzzle, I felt ready for the coldness of the water, for the shock of it on my skin.

Antoinette was already floating around in the shallow end by the time I got down there. The pool itself was glowing blue, lit from below by underwater lights, and the sky above was filled with bright stars, and the air around us was very dry and still, making everything feel a little surreal. Antoinette had brought out a bottle of champagne from the kitchen, and as I took off my shorts and T-shirt, she floated over toward the side of the pool where she'd left it.

"After tonight I'm not going to drink anymore for like a month, okay?" She laughed then and grabbed the champagne and took a sip. "You can hold me to that."

"I will," I said, and smiled at her as I slid in the water.

The water felt good on my skin, and for a moment my mind seemed to settle down, seemed to calm in a way it hadn't in several days. I submerged my head underwater and then held my breath, and when I came back up, a few seconds later, Antoinette was gone.

I called out to her, but she didn't answer. Then I heard some rustling in the cabana house and a moment later she emerged with two foam rafts, which she carried over to the pool and slid into the water.

I climbed on top of one, and she climbed on top of the other, and then we both paddled out toward the middle of the pool where we turned over and lay on our backs.

Antoinette had brought along the champagne with her, and for a while neither of us spoke. We just passed the bottle back and forth and looked up at the stars and listened to our own breathing.

Finally, after we'd finished about half the bottle, she turned to me, almost in a conspiratorial way, and said, "You know, I never told either of them, Alan. I never told them that I called you."

"Who?"

"His parents."

I looked at her.

"In case you were feeling guilty about it," she said. "They never thought that you were coming up to help out that weekend, so they weren't disappointed or anything. Nobody was. I just thought you should know."

I nodded. I had been feeling guilty about this and probably would for some time, though I didn't say that then. Instead, I just turned back toward the sky and took another sip of the champagne and then closed my eyes. In the distance, from somewhere inside the house, I could hear the faint sound of the music Antoinette had put on earlier, something light and ambient, something warm. I turned back to her.

"Can I ask you something?" I said finally.

"Of course."

"Did he ever talk about me in the past few months? Me or my wife?"

She nodded. "He talked about you guys all the time," she said. "But yes, especially in the past year."

I took the champagne as she passed it to me and put it to my lips.

"And, of course, he worried about you guys, too."

I looked at her. "About us staying together, you mean?"

"Yes." She nodded. "I think he thought that the two of you should try to have children."

"Really?" I laughed.

"Yes," she said and smiled.

I passed the bottle back to her and waited for her to take a sip. In the distance, I could see the sky lightening, the first hints of dawn on the horizon.

"And he probably told you about Tanya and him, right? Before she and I were dating?"

"Yes."

"Tanya always said that it was nothing, but I wonder."

"I don't think it was *nothing*," Antoinette said and smiled. "But who knows?"

I nodded.

I shifted on the raft and looked at her. And I thought then for the first time that weekend about how beautiful she and Daniel had been as a couple, how beautiful they'd looked together those two times I'd seen them in San Antonio, at least, and then I thought for some reason about Daniel himself and how frightened he must have been had he in fact been lost on that trail, how impossible that must have been, having to accept the reality that he would never be found, that nobody out there was coming to get him.

I closed my eyes and let the water suspend me for a while, let myself float there, and then finally I looked back at Antoinette.

"You know," I said after a moment. "You never answered the question I asked you yesterday."

"Which one?"

"About what you're going to do after you leave here, after you pack up the house."

She shrugged. "Well, maybe because I don't know." She looked out beyond the blur of the vanishing pool edge, where you could see the faint lights of distant cars on the interstate. It occurred to me then that I'd have to get on the road in a few hours, that I had morning classes to teach on Monday. I took the bottle as she passed it to me and took a long sip.

"I don't think I'd want to be anywhere else, though, not right now." She said this faintly, quietly, and then she reached over and squeezed my hand, just gently, and let it go.

I passed the bottle back to her, and then closed my eyes again. I could feel my body loosening now, everything going soft. I thought of Tanya back in San Antonio, and what I'd say to her when I returned, what would happen to us now. And I thought about Daniel and how profoundly I missed him already, how profoundly I missed his face, and how already it seemed impossible to imagine my life without him. My dear friend. My dear, dear friend, who had lucked out in so many other ways in his life and then been dealt this one bad hand. It seemed so unfair to me that he was not with us, that we were here, in his beautiful pool, and he was not.

I finally opened my eyes and turned back to Antoinette and saw that she was staring right at me. She wasn't smiling at me, but she didn't seem sad either. She was just staring at me, and I gathered that she was probably thinking what I was thinking, that we had just spent these two very strange days together, and that after I left we would probably never see each other again. There would be no reason for that to happen, after all, and yet for now, we still had about a half hour or so before that happened, a half hour or so to pretend, a half hour to float here on our backs in the darkness, in silence, but together, a half hour before the sun came up, and the darkness faded, and we would realize, with something like fear, that we had to leave.

A C K N O W L E D G M E N T S

My deepest thanks to my wonderful agent, Terra Chalberg, for her
unwavering support and advocacy over the years, and to my brilliant
editor, Diana Tejerina Miller, for her wisdom, attention, and care
with these stories. I feel so fortunate to work with both of you.

Thank you also to the many other people at Knopf who helped
to bring this book into the world: John Gall, Fred Chase, Nicole
Pedersen, Zuleima Ugalde, Maria Carella, Zachary Lutz, Matthew
Sciarappa, Amy Hagedorn, Jordan Pavlin, and Reagan Arthur.

Special thanks to Ladette Randolph, Emily Nemens, Michael
Koch, Steven Schwartz, Elizabeth McKenzie, Tom Jenks, and Mimi
Kusch, for their guidance on earlier versions of these stories, and
to the literary magazines in which many of the stories in this book
first appeared: *Ploughshares, The Southern Review, Epoch, Narra-*

tive, Colorado Review, Boulevard, Chicago Quarterly Review, Sonora Review, and *New Letters.*

I am forever indebted to my former teachers Marilynne Robinson, James Alan McPherson, David Wong Louie, Barry Hannah, and Frank Conroy, and to my dearest writer friends, Amber Dermont, Holiday Reinhorn, and Jonathan Blum, whose work is a constant source of inspiration to me and whose advice and counsel over the years has meant more to me than I can possibly express.

The stories in this collection could not have been written without the generous support of Trinity University and my colleagues in the Department of English, and I would like to give a special thanks to my partners in crime in Creative Writing, Jenny Browne and Kelly Grey Carlisle, for their kindness and friendship.

To my mother and father for filling our house with books and instilling in me a love of stories from a young age, and to my brother and sister, Mike and Di, thank you for being such wonderful siblings.

To my children, Charlotte and Alex, I love you both so much, you are my lights, and this book is for you.

And finally, most of all, to my wife and my best friend, Jenny Rowe, who has seen these stories from their earliest drafts and who is a constant source of encouragement, kindness, and love. I feel so lucky to have met you and to get to spend this life with you.

A Note About the Author

Andrew Porter is the author of the story collection *The Theory of Light and Matter* and the novel *In Between Days*. A graduate of the Iowa Writers' Workshop, he has received a Pushcart Prize, a James Michener/Copernicus Fellowship, and the Flannery O'Connor Award for Short Fiction. His work has appeared in *One Story, The Threepenny Review, Ploughshares, Narrative, The Southern Review,* and on National Public Radio's *Selected Shorts.* Currently, he teaches fiction writing and directs the creative writing program at Trinity University in San Antonio, Texas.

A Note on the Type

The text of this book was set in Electra, a typeface designed by W. A. Dwiggins (1880–1956). This face cannot be classified as either modern or old style. It is not based on any historical model, nor does it echo any particular period or style. It avoids the extreme contrasts between thick and thin elements that mark most modern faces, and it attempts to give a feeling of fluidity, power, and speed.

Composed by Digital Composition, Berryville, Virginia
Printed and bound by Berryville Graphics, Berryville, Virginia
Designed by Maria Carella